Adella's ENEMY

Jacqui Nelson

Copyright © 2013 by Jacqui Nelson
All rights reserved under International and Pan-American Copyright Conventions

By payment of required fees, you have been granted the *non*-exclusive, *non*-transferable right to access and read the text of this book. No part of this text may be reproduced, transmitted, downloaded, decompiled, reverse engineered, or stored in or introduced into any information storage and retrieval system, in any form or by any means, whether electronic or mechanical, now known or hereinafter invented without the express written permission of copyright owner.

Please Note

The reverse engineering, uploading, and/or distributing of this book via the internet or via any other means without the permission of the copyright owner is illegal and punishable by law. Please purchase only authorized electronic editions, and do not participate in or encourage electronic piracy of copyrighted materials. Your support of the author's rights is appreciated

No part of this book may be reproduced or transmitted in any form or by any electronic or mechanical means, including photocopying, recording or by any information storage and retrieval system, without the written permission of the publisher, except where permitted by law.

Thank you.

Cover design by The Killion Group
http://thekilliongroupinc.com

Chapter 1

Emporia, Kansas
March 28, 1870

Standing on the fringe of a courtyard full of women, Adella Willows waited to make a bargain with the Devil. Not that the Devil himself was coming to meet her. He was sending a fat, yellow-bellied Yankee senator dressed in a suit as fine as President Grant's.

Senator Mansfield Moreton finally sauntered out of Emporia's most stately building and through the now disbanding suffrage rally. He passed Adella and her tripod camera without a glance, so close that even out of the corner of her eye she glimpsed the silver in his mutton-chop whiskers.

Adella didn't turn her camera to follow

him. She wasn't here for a picture. Her camera was only a ruse to throw off anyone watching, as was her decision to keep her back to the senator. Both she and the senator knew this meeting was best kept clandestine. But her inability to see him made the skin between her shoulder blades itch as if a sniper's rifle were aimed at her back.

Leaving her camera facing the thinning crowd, she draped the cloth hood over her arm and set a spare lens atop the camera to catch the senator's reflection. He'd settled his heavy frame on the bench behind her and to her left. His image was distorted and unearthly, as if she viewed him through Alice's looking-glass.

"You don't really believe in all this equality for the masses, do you?" he asked her, angling his body away from her so he appeared to be watching the women departing the square with their "right to vote" picket signs.

She busied herself packing the rest of her equipment. "I'm a photographer with the *Atlanta Intelligencer*." The lie flowed unbidden from her lips—a force of habit. The truth that followed came more slowly. "I believe only in my next assignment, the one that's in your best interest to support."

The senator snorted a laugh. "My contacts said you could be blunt. You talk like an equal or worse, a superior. The Union may have freed the slaves and one day may grant women the vote, but mankind will never be equal. We are different. We are individuals. That's what has brought you to Emporia. You hold a grudge against an individual, a very long-standing grudge."

Her hands froze. But her gaze darted to the lens.

The senator's regard remained on the last lingering protestors. "The war's been over for five years," he added.

"The war's over for the dead, not for their families." Her voice sounded only slightly high-pitched, thank Dixie.

Aiming for a nonchalance she did not feel, she lifted the camera hood from the crook of her arm and pretended great interest in smoothing out its wrinkles before folding the cloth in half. "Too many soldiers, on both sides, suffered needlessly to pad the pockets of the wealthy."

"Ah, once again we speak of an individual—a prisoner of war who died a month before Lee's surrender."

Pain sliced her heart like a saber strike, swift and merciless. The war had stolen her home and her youth. She'd been fifteen when the fighting started. All of that was forgivable. The loss in that final month was not. Declan— She must not think of him.

She must focus on the task at hand. Concentrating on keeping her hands steady, she finished folding the hood.

"I've been checking up on you, Miss Willows." The senator propped one ankle on his knee and laid his intertwined fingers over his round gut. "Why do you think you're here and not some other agent?"

"I'm here because the law won't prosecute a prominent northern businessman who illegally sold rations meant for Confederate prisoners of war." She knew this well, had witnessed it firsthand. Rich Yankees—even ones supposedly assigned to deal out justice—only took care of each other. For her there hadn't been any justice, which told her that if she didn't look out for herself, no one else would.

And Senator Moreton? She'd thought he was here to increase his already ample wealth. But maybe helping her ruin Levi Parsons was also retaliation for a business deal gone wrong or a political slight. Did Moreton hold a grudge against Parsons as well?

Watching Moreton closely, she asked, "Why did you give me the document incriminating Parsons?"

The senator's image shimmered. The line of his shoulders and the angle of his jaw suddenly radiated tension. "To determine how far you're willing to go—off the books, of course. You've known Parsons was responsible for your brother's death for a week. But the judge still struts around unscathed."

Anger stiffened Adella's spine. She pushed the emotion into a far corner of her heart and made herself relax. "I won't become a murderer like Parsons, if that's what you're wondering. Death is too quick. I wish to bleed Parsons dry, but only of his precious greenbacks. Tell me, Senator Moreton, why do you think you're here and not some other government bigwig?"

"Me? What the blazes are you talking about? I organized this meeting, not you."

She set the hood on the leather valise that she always kept close at hand. Inside was the document Moreton had given her. The proof she'd searched so long to find. The form named Parsons as the ration contractor for Camp Douglas.

She raised her chin and focused solely on the senator's reflection. "You and Parsons are business partners promoting the Missouri, Kansas and Texas Railroad."

He shrugged. "That's common knowledge."

"But not common knowledge that you own stock in its rival, the Joy Line."

The senator's silence stretched her nerves taut.

"If Parsons fails to reach Indian Territory before the Joy Line," she continued, "he forfeits the land grants. His share prices become worthless. He'll lose a fortune. I can ensure his loss is your gain."

"How?"

"You presume to know everything, you tell me."

"You're merely a rabble rouser, a former Rebel spy turned unofficial government agent. You—" Planting both feet on the ground, he twisted round on the bench to stare at her openly. The whites of his deep-set eyes flashed in the glass. "You can provoke enough dissent to halt a railroad?"

"I need only delay its construction from reaching the border before your favored railroad. But to do so I need you to finance my efforts and keep the other agents out of my way—off the books, of course."

"I underestimated you, Miss Willows. Don't make the same mistake with others. You may scheme above the masses, but you can return to them very quickly." The senator stood and turned to leave. "Get the job done and don't get caught," he said, not looking back. "Or you might end up with a fate equal to your brother's."

Chapter 2

New Chicago, Kansas—340 miles north of the Indian Territory border
One day later

The steam whistle howled. Brakes screeched. Then the cheering of Adella's fellow passengers joined the hullabaloo as the train halted at New Chicago's station. Only a week off a ship from Ireland, the men had talked of nothing but employment and adventure at the end of the railroad line. The simplicity of their ambitions made her feel ancient beyond her twenty-four years.

Sadness squeezed her chest with the force of a thousand gloomy days rolled into one. A new town held the allure of new beginnings. But not for her. Never for her. She was only here to avenge the death of one man by ruining the life of another.

She waited until the last passenger left

the train before she followed. Her muscles protested, her body aching after sitting on the hard bench for hours. On the other side of the platform, the station—a rectangular building cobbled together from scrap wood fit only for a bonfire—wasn't any more comforting. Nor were the steps leading down to a narrow path of boards thrown over a sea of mud. Or the towering cloudbank, heavy with the scent of rain.

She might never come face to face with Levi Parsons in this rough and tumble place, but this was where she'd exact her revenge on him.

Behind her, the engine hissed, spewing one final plume of smoke. At the end of the train, a man dressed in the latest fashion of a bowler hat and a dark-blue three-piece suit descended from a private railcar. Reaching back, he helped down a woman with vibrant red hair only slightly more remarkable than her outfit. Her jacket might have been commissioned by some unknown army, but the trouser cuffs—visible under the billowing hem of her ankle-length skirt as she stepped down—could only have been inspired by a free spirit. The man offered her his arm. Then he strode toward the stairs, forcing her to keep up with his swift stride.

Adella recognized the pair from her time skulking around public events while she searched for the Yankee who'd killed Declan. Tears pricked the back of her eyes. She blinked them away. Your mission, she reminded herself, think only of your mission.

Henry Stevens, Levi Parsons' Chief of Operations, was in charge of ensuring the Katy reached the Indian Territory border before the competition. Adella was here to ensure he failed.

But why was Parsons' daughter here?

Adella made a beeline for the stairs, timing her pace so her path crossed the couple's. She knew the instant her amethyst silk dress snared Stevens' attention. His pace slowed. His gaze lowered, taking in her low-cut décolletage, corseted waist and swaying skirt—then travelled up again, pausing just a little too long on her bosom before finally finding her eyes. In her experience, people chose clothing for the wrong reasons or worse no reason at all. She'd assembled her wardrobe to trigger certain reactions.

Stevens halted, forcing Miss Parsons to do the same.

Adella's dress had done its job.

"May I be of service, Miss...?" Stevens gestured to the leather valise in her hand.

The case held her letters, and a glut of photographs and documents she'd painstakingly assembled over the last five years. Those years had been necessary to prepare for this day. So had the years preceding—the years she'd spent dressed as a boy in order to play her part for the Confederacy as a Rebel spy. In every stage of her life, she'd employed whatever tools she could.

Today, her specialty had become using information to provoke unrest. Pictures and words were powerful motivators, but only with people who had a conscience. The contents of her valise would be no help when dealing with a social climber like Stevens.

"My name is Miss Willows," she replied, keeping a firm grasp on her valise. "Thank you for your offer, but I wouldn't want to be a bother. I apologize if I seemed to be racing you to the stairs."

She widened her eyes and talked quickly to make her voice sound breathless. "As a new employee of the *Atlanta Intelligencer*, I'm just eager to record as much as possible about the railroad, and the towns springing up around it. Can you imagine being responsible for something as big as the Missouri, Kansas and...Texas Railroad?" She forced herself to stumble over the name, as if it were unfamiliar.

Stevens chuckled. "In fact I can. I'm Henry Stevens. We call this line the Katy, and I'm in charge of building her." His chest swelled with the proclamation. "And this is Miss Parsons."

Miss Parsons tilted her head, but the acknowledgement, although polite, was a tad stiff. Was Miss Parsons jealous of Stevens' interest? Adella racked her brain for a way to soothe any ruffled feathers. If Miss Parsons were annoyed with her, it would serve no purpose.

"There are so few women on the frontier. I hope you won't think it forward of me, but will you consent to calling me Adella?"

Miss Parsons' eyebrows shot up, but just for an instant. "I'll only agree," she replied, "if you call me Kate in return."

Adella admired Kate's gracious acceptance of her offer. But the surprise Kate had shown gave her pause. What kind of life had this well-to-do woman led that she expected Adella to be unfriendly?

Adella couldn't afford to be impressed or concerned about Parsons' daughter. She's your enemy's flesh and blood, she reminded herself. During the war, Parsons had been awarded the government contract to supply food to Confederate prisoners detained at Camp Douglas. The soldiers hadn't been fed. Parsons had gotten richer. Thousands of men had starved to death, including Declan. The pain and suffering her twin brother must have endured—

She quickly bottled up the grief that

threatened to engulf her again. She couldn't afford to be weak. Not now. Not ever.

"You're here to photograph the railroad, aren't you?" Kate asked. "I saw you taking pictures at the suffrage rally in Emporia."

Alarm hit Adella like a mule kick to the forehead. What else had Kate seen? Shoving down her panic with her grief, she recalled her activities yesterday in Emporia. She'd insisted on meeting Senator Moreton after the rally. She'd chosen the bench on the edge of the square, so they'd be less noticeable. She'd been careful. *Liar*, she reproached herself. She'd agreed to the meeting with less than her usual forethought, because she wanted the senator to support her mission.

Had Kate seen them? Best to find out immediately. Best to be bold. Best to bluff.

She plastered a smile on her face and dredged her mind for a pleasant memory to make it appear genuine. "Were you there at the end of the rally? I could have taken your picture too."

"I had to leave early to luncheon with my father," Kate replied.

Then Kate hadn't seen her with the senator. *Thank Dixie.* Adella's smile became real.

"It must be rewarding," Kate continued, "capturing such monumental moments in our nation's evolution."

"We race toward change. I can only hope that certain transformations arrive before others, and that I am present when they do." Adella bowed her head, striving to not only appear humble but to gather her wits.

She was doing more than hoping. She was making sure the changes she wanted happened. But if she wished to shape the future—to revenge Declan's death and make up for failing him during the war—she must exercise greater caution in the present. It wouldn't do to have Kate uncover her real purpose for being here. The information gathering should only flow one way. Information like why Parsons' very observant daughter was in New Chicago.

"Are you in town for a visit?" she asked.

Kate raised her chin. "A business endeavor."

"We'll discuss that later," Stevens muttered.

Pink flared across Kate's cheeks. It was hard to tell if it came from embarrassment or anger. Kate gestured toward the train. "You'll want to get a photograph of the new engine."

Stevens was suddenly all smiles. "Yes. Why don't you come by my railcar tomorrow? I can show you how best to photograph the Katy. Surely your newspaper, or you, could use the donation

I'm willing to bestow for a favorable article."

Kate's fingers tightened on his arm. "Buying good will isn't the same as creating good will."

Adella held her tongue, waiting for the pair to reveal more insights into their personalities.

Stevens patted Kate's hand. "I'm neglecting my duties. It's time I secured you a room at the hotel." He tipped his bowler to Adella. "Until tomorrow, Miss Willows."

The formality of calling her by her surname wasn't lost on her. Stevens knew the power of words and money. But he didn't seem to know the power in a woman. That could make him an easier nut to crack than the complex creature that was Kate Parsons. Although a frown marred Kate's brow, she let Stevens steer her down the stairs toward town.

Adella's thoughts spun with ideas for using the friction between the pair to delay the railroad's construction. What was their relationship? Whatever it was, it was a bonus she hadn't expected when she approached them. But that was for tomorrow, as Stevens had rightfully said.

They weren't the only people in New Chicago she could use to stall construction. If the Katy lost the race, Parsons' stock would plummet. He'd lose everything he valued. Parsons had destroyed the one thing she cherished, so she'd do the same to him. Parsons still had family but, judging from her research on him, he only seemed to care about wealth and power. When she was done with his railroad, he'd have little left.

She crossed the now empty platform to the station's solitary window. The porter had left her trunks next to it, but he was nowhere to be seen. Standing under the sagging eave, she cupped her hand against the glass, and leaned close to peer at the shadowy interior.

"Look lively," a deep Irish brogue boomed.

She flattened her spine against the station's wall. Its uneven surface jabbed her in a dozen uncomfortable places. She didn't move.

Footsteps pounded up the stairs, making the boards shudder beneath her feet. Then a lone man bounded up the last step and across the platform, his attention fixed on the train. From his shaggy hair to his massive back to his powerfully built limbs he was a series of shades of brown. She squinted. He was covered in mud.

"Hop to, lads," he hollered. "We're late!"

A dozen men raced up the steps, swarming the platform like ants summoned from the earth to capture a hill. Brown ants. They shared their leader's coloring. Like him, they were caked in mud so thick it covered them like a second skin, like armor on toy soldiers cast from the same mold...except they were the varying size and shape of ordinary men. All save their leader. Nothing ordinary about that one. With the height and muscular breadth of a giant, he towered over everyone.

The men who'd arrived with her on the train returned. They shuffled up the steps at a much slower pace. Startling clean standing next to the mud-covered men, they clustered together and darted glances at the big Irishman.

He crossed his arms and turned to face them. "Supply master usually meets new recruits rather than letting you wander off. Informed me last minute he had another task requiring his attention. Every delay means less track laid at day's end. So we're moving fast to make it up. Some of the McGrady Gang—" he gestured to the dozen mud-caked men, "—will show you how to uncouple Stevens' railcar."

Two men leapt between the cars. Metal clanged and scraped.

"Pay attention. You'll all take a turn eventually. When they're done, jump aboard the train. It's time to earn your pay."

"But we've been travelin' since dawn," one of the new recruits grumbled.

"And you'll work every day from dawn till dusk," the big Irishman replied. "Welcome to the life of railroader, boyo. You'll get used to it soon enough."

"It's not me that needs convincing, it's me arse."

All of the workmen broke out in guffaws. Their leader didn't join them. Then a deafening squeal came from the front of the train. The laughter died as they spun as one to face the sound.

The platform was barely long enough to provide access to the two passenger cars. Between those cars and the engine stood a stockcar piled high with the iron rails used to form the track. A man, wearing loose fitting railroad bibs and a wide-brimmed hat drawn low over his face, crouched on top of the rails. The workmen—both clean and muddy—surged to the edge of the platform, blocking her view.

"It's one of the Joy Men." The declaration came from the big Irishman hidden somewhere beyond the wall of bodies between her and the train.

A spy for the rival railroad? If James Joy had sent a rabble rouser from his line, she'd best learn as much about him as possible. Starting with what he looked like.

She pushed through the workmen. Each

man spun with a scowl, ready to berate whoever poked him in the ribs or stepped on his toes. When they saw her, they stumbled back, jaws dropping. She reached the platform's edge just in time to see the man on the stockcar leap to the engine, run across its back and slide down the cattle guard to the ground.

"After him, lads!" The big Irishman roared from somewhere close.

She turned but didn't see him. The men she did see stood frozen, their gazes locked on her.

Their leader shoved through them with a growl. "Why aren't you—?" He slammed to a halt in front of her. He hadn't touched her, but the sight of him looming over her with a combination of anger and disbelief twisting his mud-streaked face, pushed her back. She teetered on the edge of the platform, the weight of her valise throwing her further off balance. Many hands reached for her, including the giant's.

She refused to let go of her valise and accept them.

She fell with a shriek. Her rear end hit the mud with a bruising wallop. She gritted her teeth to stop any additional embarrassing outbursts then, valise still in hand, staggered to her feet. And promptly sank ankle deep in the muck.

Galloping hoof beats splashed the sodden

earth behind her. She could only assume the man had found a horse and was making his retreat. Instinctively, she tried to give chase. The mud held her feet prisoner. *Blast it to Hell.* All she could do was stare over her shoulder and watch the man ride pell-mell out of town, his floppy-brimmed hat waving goodbye.

A colossal groan rent the air. She jerked round to face the train, as did the men on the platform above her. The terrible sound came again, making the stockcar shudder with its force. A crack like gunfire echoed. Chains burst. Iron screeched against iron. And the mountain of rails toppled toward her. Trapped as she was in the muck below, she'd soon be crushed in a muddy grave. Fear devoured all further thought.

A broad hand clamped round her arm and yanked. Her feet popped from the mud, and she sailed through the air before landing on the platform. The hand released her. Shock rendered her legs useless, crumpling her like a rag doll on the boards beside her valise.

With the force of Thor's hammer, the first rail struck the earth. A shower of mud pelted the platform on either side of her. The clanging that followed left her ears ringing.

"Did I hurt you?" the now familiar brogue whispered, so close it raised goose flesh.

Lifting her head, she stared into eyes as silver as newly minted dollars, the only difference in a face as muddy as the rest. The man's massive frame crouched protectively over her. She was bombarded with memories of her mother's stories, tales passed down for generations of legendary Celtic warriors. She had never dreamed of encountering one of those mythical men in human form.

He reached out to touch her.

"She all right, Mac?"

The question halted his hand. He stood, taking his warmth with him.

"Are you daft?" His tone had gone from hushed moorland stream to storm-tossed sea. "Why were you standing so close to the platform edge? What kind of harebrained lass loiters around a rail platform rather than heading straight into town?"

She pushed to her feet, ignoring his outstretched hand when he bent to assist her. Instead, she clenched her valise with both hands. "I was unaware certain areas of New Chicago were off limits."

His brows slanted at an unforgiving angle. "Maybe they should be. You could've been killed."

She glanced at the dozen muddy men, hovering close behind him. He'd called them the McGrady Gang. They were nodding, their faces etched with concern. Chivalry from a band of dirt-poor and dirt-covered Irish laborers? Once again, the new recruits stood back. Watching and waiting.

Their leader continued frowning, this time in the direction the rider had disappeared. "Should'a stopped him. Now my men will have to work double, loading those rails and unloading them at the worksite."

Ah. Now he revealed his true self. He wasn't as worried about her as he was about his work and his men. This she could understand and use.

"Sorry to be such a bother." She lowered her gaze and tried to appear contrite, which wasn't difficult as she truly regretted seeing anyone involved in such back-breaking labor. But being a bother was her job. Now she must become even more bothersome. She must embrace every opportunity to delay this construction crew from reaching the border.

Her Irish rescuer exhaled a weary breath and said in a much gentler tone, "'Tisn't your fault. Don't worry about us."

"Oh, but I do. And to apologize for seeing your men's lives made more difficult, I promise to buy each and every one of them a drink tonight."

A round of hoorays went up.

"Now, lass, you needn't—"

"I must."

"Miss, it's not necessary—"

"It is."

"Look, lady, I can't let—"

"You can. And you can call me Miss Willows."

"Stubborn English," he muttered.

Annoyance made her squeeze her valise's handle even tighter. "I'm not English. I'm American."

"Isn't Willows an English name?"

She opened her mouth, then snapped it shut. She wondered if she might wrench the handle from her valise, so tight had her grip become.

His eyes narrowed even more. "If you've got something to say, Miss Willows, say it."

"You're overbearing and opinionated—an Irishman I heard all about in my youth." Her mother's tales of her home country hadn't always been admiring.

Behind him, the McGrady Gang hooted in mirth. "She's put ye in yer place, Mac."

She felt no pleasure in the accomplishment. It served no purpose. Unfortunately, she was struggling to recall her purpose. Her befuddlement had arrived with the big Irishman, the one the men called Mac. Her reaction to him was dangerous. He was dangerous.

Refusing to look at him, she stared at the train. She was here to delay construction of the track, so Parsons lost the race and his ill-gotten gains. She was here for Declan.

"Mr. Mac, I—"

"Cormac."

She couldn't stop her gaze from returning to him.

"That's my name." He glanced away as if he suddenly didn't want to look at her either. "My friends call me Mac."

A stab of regret robbed her of a reply. She forced herself to welcome the hurt. She wasn't here to make friends, so she should be happy that he didn't number her among his. In her line of work, friendships never helped. Too much guilt came with them.

Hurried footsteps rattled the stairs. Cormac installed himself between her and whoever approached.

"What the devil's going on, McGrady?" Despite the voice being clipped and angry, she recognized its owner as the previously sugar-toned Henry Stevens. "I hired you to save time," he barked, "not squander it." Stevens' footsteps grew louder, heading toward the platform edge.

Cormac's hands fisted at his sides. He shifted sideways with Stevens. Without a word, the McGrady Gang moved as well. Cormac McGrady and the men named after him formed a tight circle around her, keeping her hidden.

Did they worry what Stevens might say

if he saw her among them?

"Everything's under control." Cormac's voice was firm, resuming the tone he'd used when he'd first rallied his workers. "Someone broke the chains and dumped the load."

"One of the Joy Men?" Stevens asked.

"Who else? You got problems with other folks you haven't told me about?" A note of challenge had crept into Cormac's tone. But when he didn't receive an answer, he merely shrugged. "All I know for certain is the man left us with more work." His gaze shifted to the new recruits. "Into the mud, lads, and put those rails back where they belong."

Hesitant footsteps scraped the platform. Voices grumbled. The platform shook. Mud splashed. More of the same followed, intensifying the grumbling. But Cormac and the McGrady Gang remained rooted around her like silent oaks. Only when Stevens' swift stride stomped off, did they turn and begin jumping into the mud as well.

Cormac paused on the platform's edge with his back to her. When the last of his men were on the ground and out of earshot, he said, "Don't come to the saloon tonight. 'Tis a place unfit for a lady. I'll make sure my men get what you promised. I'll make up for their pains. I'm responsible for them, not you."

Before she could argue, he jumped down and helped his men move the rails. The thick muscles along his shoulders and arms bulged with the effort. He would make a powerful adversary.

She'd never backed away from a challenge. Contrary to Cormac's order, she'd buy her promised round in person, because she wanted to buy several more afterward. She'd set up her first act of disruption. Men who over-indulged in drink during the night suffered the following morning and worked much slower.

She wasn't so sure about Celtic warriors. A shiver danced across her skin, as she watched Cormac labor with the strength of three men. The only thing to do was use his brawn to aid her mission. The image of his large hands clenching into fists as Stevens tried to march around him, leapt to mind. If she could incite a brawl tonight, then tomorrow's progress would be even slower.

All she had to do was find the right words while coaxing the right number of drinks into the workmen and their leader.

Chapter 3

Careful to keep his clean clothing—and his even cleaner self—out of the muck, Cormac followed the wooden footpath that led from the bathhouse to Eden's. Ahead, the hushed darkness surrounding the saloon amplified the noise within: coarse language, loud laughter and dreadful music played on an out-of-tune piano by a tone-deaf musician. How he longed for a traditional *céilí* in Ireland. But if a man wanted a drink in New Chicago, he went to Eden's.

That's where the McGrady Gang would be. Since leaving his sister, Meghan, with her new family two months ago, his gang was the closest thing he had to kin. He'd promised to buy them a round of drinks. He'd promised a very pretty lass with eyes like amber gems. A promise he suddenly wished he hadn't made. Her safety was top priority, but he longed to lose himself in those amazing eyes again.

Under some misguided notion of helping, Miss Willows had offered to compensate his men with drink. He had no idea why Americans did half the things they did, so he'd given her a way out. He wouldn't see her tonight. Despite knowing this, he paused in the saloon doorway and scanned the room. The disappointment weighing his shoulders deepened, heavier than the longest workday. No auburn-haired spitfire swathed in purple silk. No lass above him in dress, manners, and prospects.

Now that Meghan no longer needed him, his sole purpose was to see the Katy built to the border with no one killed in the process. Too many in Galway had died because of him. He wouldn't let that happen here.

But if he didn't catch the bloody saboteur who'd been harassing the railroad for weeks with rapidly mounting violence— His heart still seized at the memory of Miss Willows nearly crushed under a ton of cascading steel. Resignation joined the load on his shoulder. It snuffed out the lonely ember of yearning that had arrived with today's train. He'd been right to insist Miss Willows stay away.

His gaze sought out the McGrady Gang. He might refer to all of the Katy's workers as his men, but only one group was his gang. Formed during his five years working on the transcontinental railroad, the McGrady Gang hadn't given him any choice in the matter, not even in their name. Tonight his gang wasn't carousing with the women, or distracting the new recruits with questions about life back in Ireland, or tiring out the other gangs with arm-twisting challenges. They clustered silently around a table in the back.

What were they up to?

Behind the bar, Eden beckoned him with an elegant tilt of her chin, making the glossy dark curls piled atop her head shimmer. While he took a stool opposite her, she poured him a glass from one of the better bottles of rotgut found in the West. Then she raised her coffee mug to him in salute.

He couldn't contain the grimace that followed his first swallow. The memory of good Irish whiskey lingered on his tongue, reminding him of his failures. He couldn't pay back the dead. His trip home to Galway had shown that he couldn't even pay back the living.

"To bitter days and better nights," Eden said, taking a sip of her coffee. "And to sweet dreams."

He grimaced again. He hadn't meant to share his dreams with Eden, but that's what men did. In her mid-twenties, Eden was younger than half of the girls under her charge. But she ran her saloon, and the brothel above it, with a shrewdness that belied her age and hinted of a history heavy enough to double her years.

Whatever her past, Eden seemed to have mastered the present. Instead of taking men to her bed, she stayed downstairs and took their confessions. Eden kept their deepest secrets. Everything else the men told her, or she overheard, was fair game. She enjoyed giving advice but also enjoyed taking her own sweet time. When this happened, her pale-green eyes sparkled. Right now her eyes blazed with fireworks. She had pertinent information that concerned him.

He sent an inquiring glance toward his gang.

"Chess," she replied. "They liberated your board from your tent an hour ago."

"And to think I almost tossed it in the Atlantic coming back. Never expected they'd remember the game so fondly."

Eden shrugged, then picked up a glass and polished it. The corners of her ruby lips curled ever so slightly.

"Eden..." He scrubbed his hand over his jaw. "Cut me some line. My day's been harder than usual."

"You suffered a mishap at the station," said a voice as raspy as an old saw. Floyd, the railroad's telegraph operator, sidled up next to him. Despite his occupation, or maybe because of it, the grizzled man had a propensity for spouting secrets like a leaky rain barrel.

Propping an elbow on the bar, Cormac turned to face him. "Tell me something I don't know."

Floyd waggled his glass at him. Cormac gestured for Eden to fill it.

The old man downed the drink and smacked his lips. "Tonight the stakes of yonder game have grown. Still, whatever the outcome I'm happy." Contrary to his proclamation he frowned at the once more empty glass in his hand.

Cormac waved impatiently for Eden to top him up.

"Very kind of you. And them," Floyd added, gesturing to the McGrady Gang. "Whoever loses, buys drinks for everyone, including me."

A jolt straightened Cormac's spine. Could it be Miss Willows? No. He'd told her not to— He spat out a curse. Growing up with five sisters hadn't taught him a thing. "Who's buying?"

"Not yer men. So far they've won three matches. Still, I think they're pondering their opponent more than their playing. From their silence, their luck's run out. They'll be buying the next round. Which is good—" Floyd nudged his glass toward

Eden, "—'cause I'm empty again."

Cormac slammed his palm on the counter between them. "Tell me who you're talking about."

"Sorry, Mac. The lady's new to me. Don't know her name." Floyd edged away until he disappeared into the crowd.

Shoving Cormac's hand off the counter, Eden retrieved Floyd's glass and deposited it in a washbasin. "Good God, these days you're as grumpy as an old bear."

Cormac hunched his shoulders. "She shouldn't be here."

Eden released a very unladylike snort. "And where should she be, Cormac McGrady? I don't know much about the woman, having only exchanged names with her, but she's welcome in my saloon anytime. Adella Willows is dandy for business."

Anticipation and guilt struck a double blow dead center in his chest. He shouldn't be happy she was here. If she got hurt—

A whisper-light touch brushed his arm. The tough-as-nails madam's grasp was so gentle a child could've pulled away. But the unexpected flash of compassion that crossed Eden's beautiful face was what held him in place. He hadn't even realized he'd jumped to his feet.

"Go easy, Mac," she murmured. "Allow your men to embrace life even if you can't."

Then she released him and sauntered off to pour her next customer a drink.

Cormac forced himself to traverse the saloon slowly. How did one *go easy* when one's heart was racing like a runaway train? He stopped behind his gang and raked his fingers through his damp hair, suddenly thankful he'd taken time after scrubbing out the mud to comb the thick tangles.

"This game is delightful." Adella's voice drifted through the knot of men with the unhurried drawl of a southerner. "As is your company."

"Yer just saying that 'cause yer winning now," one of his men replied.

"Serves you right for being such excellent teachers." Her voice flowed like water, softening the sharp tongue she'd used so effectively on him just hours earlier. "My compliments to whoever taught you."

"Mac did. Played every night before..."

He strained to hear more. But the only sound, other than the continuous jabber of the saloon patrons outside the circle of his gang, was the faint click of chess pieces.

"Before?" Adella finally prompted.

"Before leaving us."

"And saying he wouldn't be back. Ever."

More silence followed his gang's gruff replies.

"So," Adella said, drawing out the word until his skin tingled and his clothes felt too tight. "He doesn't play chess with you anymore. And, as can be inferred by his absence, he doesn't socialize with you either. What does he do?"

To have her discuss him so casually, even in an admonishing tone, filled him with unexpected pleasure. It was that damned voice of hers. It made everything she said sound good. Even after five years laying track over a half-a-dozen states, he hadn't heard its match.

"Mac will get here soon as he's put the railroad to bed."

"Never asks a man to work longer than him."

"Or harder. Ye saw him. He wore as much mud as us."

Each time one of his men spoke, their tone grew increasingly earnest, as if trying to make up for their previous surliness.

"Is your work always so laborious?" she asked. "And so...dirty?"

His men laughed, their gravity gone. She'd known just how to take it away.

"This mornin' we introduced a stick of dynamite to the banks of a wee gully, levelin' it out. Not the best way to lay track, but the fastest. They hired us to be quick."

"The cloud of earth thrown into the air rained down on us somethin' fierce. We got the worst of it."

"The McGrady Gang always does, 'cause we're always at the front."

This time Cormac laughed with his gang. They spun and fell back as if they'd never heard his laugh. Maybe they hadn't. He couldn't remember the last time.

Adella sat with her hand hovering over her queen. Ready, with the support of her bishop, to take her opponent's king. Her dress, this one a vibrant green, drew a man's attention to the pale swell of her bosom. His gaze continued upward, over the slender curve of her neck, her delicately parted lips and higher. He searched for greater treasure.

In the flickering lantern light, the amber of her eyes glowed like gold at the end of a rainbow, promising untold riches. And many secrets. And one revelation. It wasn't merely the color of her eyes that mesmerized him. It was the way she looked at him, as if he was the only man in the room.

Eden's advice rang in his head. *Go Easy.* Not even growing up in a house full of sisters offered a clue to his next move with Adella. His gaze drifted to her hand still hovering over the chessboard. That game he knew. Each move told volumes. As did the moves not taken.

He gestured toward the piece she'd yet to

move. "That's checkmate. I think you play chess better than you let on."

She jerked back her hand, abandoning her victory, retreating. No. He wouldn't let her. He shook his head, remembering all of Eden's counsel. *Allow your men to embrace life even if you can't.* Suddenly, he wanted to embrace life with nothing held back. Not only did he want the Katy to win the race in order to keep his men employed, he wanted Adella. The realization made him as eager as the greenest recruit in town. It also scared the hell out of him, because he realized something else.

Adella had plans of her own, plans that didn't include him, plans she was hiding. She hadn't stood on the edge of the platform because she was daft. She hadn't ventured into a rowdy saloon to buy drinks under a misguided notion of helping. And she certainly wasn't playing chess with his men for the fun of it.

Why was she in New Chicago? Most people came for the railroad. A railroad he needed to protect. His conscience demanded he honor that commitment, but his entire being vibrated with an even greater urge to keep Adella safe.

What could a woman like Adella want with the railroad? There was only one way to find out.

"At this point, Miss Willows, retreat isn't

an option," he said. "For either of us."

Astonishment stole the air from Adella's lungs. The deep brogue was familiar. The man standing before her was not. How could Cormac McGrady look so different but still confound her so completely?

"You've won," he said, "but I'm still buying the round. You'll find I'm stubborn about keeping promises."

"Your hair," she blurted. Apparently she had enough air to speak, just not sensibly.

"What about it?" He ran his fingers through the thick waves, doing what her fingers ached to do. Hair, so dark that it rivaled the night, had been hidden under all that dull brown mud. It made his silver eyes all the more intense. He stared at her, unblinking, demanding her answer.

It would serve no purpose to have him catch her staring in return.

She lowered her gaze. "It's...different."

Amazingly, he laughed again. The sound was so resonant it vibrated in her bones and sent her thoughts swooping like swallows over a barn. Ah yes, this was the giant who so easily made her forgot she had plans beyond him. She lifted her chin and studied him. She was, she told herself, only examining him to better learn how to overcome him.

The square line of his jaw was smooth, freshly shaven. The ample, sun-burnished muscles of his neck led down to a linen shirt. His sleeves were rolled up, revealing more tanned, heavily corded flesh. A waistcoat covered his broad chest and flat stomach, then snug trousers over narrow hips. The brown fabric fit him perfectly as if custom-made. No, not brown but intermingled threads of gold and russet. Homespun tweed from a distant island. Her fingers ached again. This time to learn what lay beneath such foreign fabric.

"Different," he said, nodding, "is an appropriate word for today. How do you feel?"

She blinked. "Feel?"

"You struck the earth fairly hard when you fell."

Heat scorched her cheeks. "Oh yes. That. I am quite recovered."

"Out here, a man can usually count on a bit of rain to wash away his work. That way he doesn't come to town looking grim enough to startle ladies off train platforms. I'd say it's been a different, and difficult, day for both of us."

"You work too hard." She bit the inside of her cheek, regretting the sentiment behind her words more than the words themselves. She should only want to reduce his workload in order to delay the Katy from reaching the border, not to offer him comfort.

He shrugged. "There's no shame in an honest day's work."

"For dishonest overlords?"

A slight tightening of his brow informed her she'd struck a chord.

"Someone's told you a story or two about Ireland," he replied. "Does your informer have a name?"

"They cheat to get even richer, you know."

He allowed a heavy silence to stretch between them as if he meant to challenge her avoidance of his question. But instead he said, "They?"

"The railroad owners."

"There's good and bad in every person."

"Even in the English?"

He laughed again. The same rumbling sound that kept turning her body and mind to mush.

"I've recently been reminded to keep an open mind, even about the English." A sudden commotion on the other side of the saloon, two men exchanging blows over some unknown grievance, removed his smile.

"You shouldn't be here," he said gruffly. "It's not safe."

"It's as good a place as any." In her line of work, dangers were everywhere. Here they included a saboteur who'd almost killed her. The man had been so reckless he hadn't seemed to care if his actions hurt others. Adella would rather die than cause someone's death. The anguish she'd experienced when she'd first learned Declan had died, the relentless grief every day that followed— She couldn't put other families through what she'd felt, what she was still feeling. She couldn't live knowing she'd caused that amount of pain. Not even to get revenge on someone she despised as much as Parsons.

"Besides," she continued, pushing aside her morbid thoughts, "if I hadn't ventured inside this saloon, I wouldn't have been reminded of an interest in long-forgotten games."

"Why venture at all? Why come to New Chicago?" Cormac's gaze pierced her.

His sudden interest in her motives made her throat constrict. She forced herself not to swallow. He was waiting for a reaction— and an answer. Of course! She hadn't told him her cover story. "My newspaper sent me to photograph the railroad."

Silent and as impenetrable as a stone, he continued staring at her.

"You don't believe a woman can do the job?" She sharpened her tone, aiming to sound offended.

One of his dark brows arched. "I haven't

seen you with a camera."

Her tension eased, letting her breathe normally again. The conversation was headed in a direction she could work with. "I've had little time to unpack, what with falling off platforms and wanting to make up for causing your men more work."

"Your day hasn't been all hardships, has it? You mentioned enjoying chess. So, the least I can do is offer you another game."

"With you?" The prospect of spending more time with him sent a spark of anticipation up her spine.

"Aye, and if I win, you give your word you won't return to this saloon."

Disappointment doused her like a cloudburst. He only wanted to be rid of her. She opened her mouth to refuse, but his gang beat her to it with a chorus of no's.

"She's in a saloon..." Cormac stared each of his men in the eye until they quieted, "...with a brothel above it."

Their gazes fell like dominoes.

"Aw, Mac, she ain't in any danger."

"We've been guardin' her like hawks."

"You know she shouldn't be here," Cormac said. "Remember who we are and who we work with."

The rebuke that they didn't know her—or what she was capable of—hovered on Adella's lips. She swallowed the foolish words. They once again failed to serve her purpose. She couldn't let anyone know her strengths, good or bad.

"Del, is that you?"

Her heart slammed against her ribcage. Only two men had called her by that name. One was dead. She scrambled upright and sent her chair toppling. It struck the floor with the crack of a bullwhip.

Fergal Kilroy pushed his way through the McGrady Gang. The handsome lad from her youth—the one who'd teased her unmercifully while defending her as fiercely as her brother—had grown into a man of striking good looks. But a world-weariness that did not match his years clung to him, shadowing his once warm brown eyes and boyish face.

The reason for his pain—and for the pain she wanted to inflict upon Parsons—burst through the walls she'd erected around her past. She took a step back, gasping to draw breath, struggling to control her grief, and failing. *Miserably.*

Fergal reached for her. "Del, wait."

Cormac inserted himself once more between her and another man. "Why is she scared of you?" His voice was low, his words slow and precise. And all the more deadly for it.

Here was the work-disrupting brawl she'd hoped to instigate. Unfortunately, she no longer wanted it. Not between these two men.

"I'm not frightened," she blurted out. "I'm—" Stunned. Undone. Destroyed. None of that could happen. She straightened her shoulders. "I'm just surprised."

Fergal peered around Cormac, his gaze riveted on her, pleading. "I tried to find you after— Dec made me promise that I would. Del, I—"

"Those names are dead."

He flinched. "Adella, I never meant for Declan to—"

She raised her hands. "I don't want to talk about him. I blame myself more than you."

"You shouldn't." His gaze dipped, travelling over her dress, and his eyes widened. "My word, but you've grown into a fine lady."

"How do you know each other?" The question was casual, but Cormac's back was rigid, his hands once again fisted by his sides.

"We grew up together in Georgia." Fergal's gaze swept the men surrounding them. The beginnings of a familiar teasing grin twitched his lips. "She's a mick like us. Her people—"

"Fergal!" Adella winced. She hadn't meant to say his name so sharply. But the Fergal she'd known, once he started talking, was difficult to stop. "No one's interested in a poor southern horse trainer and his family."

"Not poor but miserly. Your father cared about horses at the cost of everything else. Stingy and stubborn, he was. A right sour ol' codger. I'm not just saying that 'cause he was born in Coventry. The best part of you is Irish. Your mother..." He released a low whistle. "Now she was a corker."

Complications. They were part of her job. But why this job? And why Fergal? She pressed her lips tight to stifle a groan. Fergal was one of the reasons her mother had told so many tales of Ireland. She'd shared them to enlighten Adella about charming young Irishmen, even those born in America and living just over the fence—on the greener side with the rich plantation owner's family.

Fergal's eyes took on a faraway look. It made him appear young again. Like the boy who'd disobeyed his father and ran wild through the fields and forests alongside her and Declan.

"Like sunshine on a dreary day, your mother was," he murmured. "She raised grand children." A shadow from the past suddenly darkened his eyes. He closed them convulsively.

The McGrady Gang were too busy grinning at her to notice.

"Mac was certain Miss Willows was

English to the bone," one of them said.

"He even told her so," added another.

Cormac's attention remained on Fergal. "I made a fool of myself based on a name I recognized...in the wrong way."

Fergal opened his eyes, his expression unreadable. "And then?"

"Miss Willows put me in my place. Then—" Cormac's voice turned gruff, "—after the saboteur nearly killed her, Stevens arrived and put us all in our places."

Fergal inhaled sharply, his gaze snapping to Adella. "That was you at the train station this afternoon?" He lifted his gaze heavenward. "Sweet Mary and Joseph, I didn't know. I should've met the new recruits like usual, instead of..."

Cormac shook his head. "Wasn't your choice. You said you had to talk with some farmers upset with the railroad. I'm surprised Stevens hasn't told me about them yet."

A clammy unease stole up her spine. "How do you know each other?" she asked, like a parrot repeating Cormac's earlier question.

"I oversaw a cut crew on the transcontinental." Fergal's gaze skimmed the McGrady Gang standing around him. "That's where I met this lot. We parted ways after that railroad held a fancy ceremony where the owners finally lifted a hammer and drove the last spike. I drifted south and eventually found the Katy and a promotion to supply master. I report to Stevens now."

Adella pressed her fingertips to her throbbing temples. If Fergal had been employed by a business in town—the hotel, a mercantile, even this saloon—she might've been able to confide in him, just a little. But he worked for the Katy. By targeting Parsons via his railroad, Adella threatened Fergal's livelihood. She was Fergal's enemy. The same held true for the McGrady Gang and Cormac.

She clutched the table for support and her gaze fell to the chessboard. Every day presented a new game, and she must play all of them alone.

"You look pale." Cormac stood beside her with her chair in his hand. "You'd best sit down."

She forced herself to push away from the table and Cormac. He reached for her arm, then stopped and stared at her in silence.

"As a walking boss," one of the McGrady Gang said, once more jumping in to fill an awkward silence, "Fergal was lousy at walking but first-rate at bossing. His leg helped him find his calling as the Katy's supply wrangler."

She spun to face Fergal. Without Cormac

standing between them, she now saw him fully.

He drew himself up, forcing his weight off a cane he'd been leaning upon. The movement made him grimace. "The sawbones said I'd die. So he didn't bother removing the bullet in the bone." He went very still. "I should have died in Camp Douglas too."

Adella forced herself to remain still as well. Fergal wouldn't welcome her pity. That didn't stop her from silently grieving for the pain he'd suffered. Not just to his leg. Her brother and Fergal had been best friends. Fergal was the reason Declan had joined the army, the reason Declan was dead. Well, one of the reasons.

If she hadn't told Declan that at fifteen he was too young to join the fighting... If she hadn't told him he was a fool for enlisting just because his best friend was of age and could... If she hadn't told him he'd regret his decision one day, and she wouldn't be there to help him... He might not have given up and stopped writing to her at the very end. He might have sent her a letter during those final months of the war. She might have saved him.

Now, she'd make Parsons pay for the loss Fergal bore as heavily as she. But she couldn't do it through men such as Fergal and the McGrady Gang. She understood that now. Retrieving her valise from under the table, she moved out of the men's sheltering circle. They had a way of doing that, rallying around her, cocooning her.

When she stood alone, she turned to address them. She was careful not to look at Fergal. Or Cormac. "The hour grows late. I must wish you goodnight." With her head held high, she marched toward the door. Outside, a chill breeze gusted in her face. She plowed into it and the darkness, following the walkway toward her hotel.

"Blasted Irish," she muttered, wrapping her free arm around her waist to ward off the cold. Except her back felt warmer than her front, as if something or someone blocked the wind.

She spun round. For once her foolish feet cooperated and found solid purchase on the boards. A pair of hefty hands took ownership of her elbows, jostling her valise out of her hand. It fell with a thud. She thrust her hand into the hidden pocket she'd sewn in her skirt.

Her breath stalled in her throat, then lodged there when her other hand slammed against rough tweed. She locked her elbow, holding the rock-solid wall of muscles behind the cloth at bay. Cormac's height and breadth filled her vision, his stomach muscles jumping beneath her palm. She clenched his waistcoat, then splayed her fingers and shoved hard with the flat of her palm. He sucked in his breath, but didn't budge.

"What were you thinking?" she demanded. "I could've shot you."

He stared down at her hand. Not the one groping him just above the trousers riding low on his hips, but the other one—the one she'd used to extract the double-barreled derringer from her skirt. A derringer she now held between them.

"Why do you own a gun?" he asked.

"I find a weapon useful for these types of situations." Despite her words, she returned the palm pistol to its hiding place and scooped up her valise. With it back in her hand, she breathed a little easier.

He muttered something in Gaelic that she didn't understand, but that rolled off his tongue as easily as only a favorite oath can.

"There's no need for foul language," she said primly.

"There's every need." His grip on her arms tightened before he released her. "It doesn't please me to learn your life is so dangerous you require a gun."

She busied herself straightening her sleeves, so she wouldn't have to meet his gaze. "And I don't like large men creeping up on me from behind and manhandling me."

"Neither do I. That's why I'm here."

There was tenseness in him that should've eased now that her gun no longer poked him in the gut. She leaned sideways just enough to peer around him. Three slovenly dressed men slouched on the steps of the saloon, watching them. They weren't from the McGrady Gang.

Cormac made a great show of offering her his arm and said more loudly than necessary, "May I escort you to your hotel, Miss Willows?"

"How very kind of you to finally ask, Mr. McGrady," she replied, accepting his arm.

The tightly leashed strength under her palm made her unduly aware of his every move. Each stride, shortened to match hers. Each breath she hoped would precede a comment that would help her regain her usual gift for idle banter. But he said nothing and the resulting silence made her incapable of any thought except how warm and safe she felt walking beside him.

The lights of her hotel came into view and his footsteps slowed. "About our chess game..."

Had he changed his mind about spending even that small amount of time with her? Damned if she'd let him reject her first. "There's no need to play that game. You were right about me being in the saloon." *Albeit for reasons different than you are pondering.* "I won't go back. You've got what you wanted."

He lowered his head toward hers. "I want...other things."

Her gullible heart thundered with hope. "Such as?" she asked, striving to sound disinterested.

"I wanted to see you home without any mishap."

"And here we are." She tried to remove her palm from his arm, but his callused hand covered hers, anchoring her to him.

"I promised you a game and, as I said before, I keep my promises."

Her mouth was too dry to answer. She turned the only thing she could, her head, and stared at the hotel. The refuge of the lobby lay within, only three steps and one door away

His breath heated her cheek as he bent even closer and whispered, "Why are you—?" He halted abruptly.

"Why am I what?"

"If I ask the wrong question, I worry you'll run away."

"You don't frighten me." The tremor running through her wasn't from fright.

He sighed. "I don't know what to believe."

"I don't return my gun to its hiding place when I'm around men who scare me." Despite her words she kept her gaze on the hotel and not him.

"Then why won't you look at me?" His tone had turned teasing.

"You're too tall," she quipped back. "It's awkward continually craning my neck to stare up at you."

Suddenly, his hands enveloped her waist and lifted her off the boardwalk. She gasped and clutched his shoulder with her free hand. But he merely set her on the top step of the hotel, so they stood eye to eye.

"Mr. McGrady—"

"Cormac."

She released his shoulder, disgusted that she'd continued holding him when he'd already let go of her. "Ah yes," she huffed, clasping her valise with both hands so she wouldn't be tempted to touch him again. "Only your friends call you Mac."

"My men call me Mac. My family called me Cormac. Or at least my sisters did." He bowed his head, like a sinner forcing himself to share a difficult confession. "They raised me. They all had names beginning with an M. They said a boy with five girls bossing him about needed something of his own, even if it was only his name."

He raised his gaze to meet hers again. "Our families shape us. Our names as well."

Nerves stretched taut, she forced herself

to hold her ground. "Fergal talks too much."

"Aye, but oddly enough he grows quieter with drink…until he reaches the point where he needs to be carried home. Twice, I've been summoned for that task. Both times he's cursed an Englishman named Willows and apologized with equal fervor to a Dec and a Del. Who I'd assumed, until now, were brothers."

A chill stronger than any change of weather stole over her. She couldn't move or speak or think.

His brow furrowed. "I've spoken out of turn. As I said, Fergal only mentioned your family twice, and he wasn't in his right mind when he did. He's a good man with more demons than most. He deserves help. Maybe you do as well."

"What do you want?" she whispered.

His frown intensified. "Tonight? Nothing." He strode down the pathway, away from her.

"Mr. McGrady," she called after him. He didn't stop. "Cormac!"

He halted and graced her with a lopsided smile that made her heart flutter in her chest. "Yes, Adella?"

"Everyone wants something."

"I'm looking forward to seeing you again, to playing our chess game."

"And what will you demand if you win?"

"That's not the game I wish to play with

you, lass."

A rush of pleasure heated her. He was indeed a dangerous opponent. "You talk in riddles."

"I want to know you better. Spending time with you will be reward enough." He stared at her as if daring her to say otherwise, which was absurd. He couldn't want her intruding into his life any more than she already had. It was merely her mind, craving things that did not exist. And if they did, they would vanish soon enough. He would spurn her if he discovered why she was in New Chicago.

Her life felt very empty. For the second time today, tears stung her eyes.

She turned her back on Cormac, before he could do the same to her, and marched into the hotel. Challenges and complications. They were everywhere. Inside her heart and out.

Chapter 4

With her camera and tripod on her shoulder and her valise in her hand, Adella picked her way along the wooden walkway in front of the clapboard and canvas buildings crowding New Chicago's streets. The morning sun peeked through clouds as gray as a blacksmith's anvil, then retreated. Another day with the threat of rain and with work to do while hemmed in by mud.

She glared at the earth surrounding her, churned up by the multitude of wagons, horses and men who slogged straight through the muck until the ground was the consistency of butter. No. More like molasses. The memory of its tenacious grip filled her thoughts, along with Cormac.

Overbearing and opinionated...and protective. If he hadn't been at the train station, she'd have—

Her foot slipped on some unseen bit of

mud transferred from sea to path. The weight of her camera threatened to topple her. She caught her balance a whisper from disgrace. Fortunately, no cracking sounds heralded a broken camera or worse a broken limb. If she fell again, Cormac wouldn't be here to pull her to safety.

Not that she needed, or wanted, his help. He just wasn't in town to do so. From her hotel room, she'd observed Cormac and his men depart before dawn on the train. She hadn't seen Stevens, but his private railcar had gone with the workers.

The town was hers to explore without any railroad men hampering her efforts to derail their project and cast Parsons into the poorhouse...if she could only keep from tumbling into the mud and having to return to the hotel. Tomorrow, it would be time to delve into her wardrobe and modify her attire. Today, she wasn't retreating. Before day's end, her champagne-colored dress would probably be spattered with mud stains. She did not care. She squared her shoulders and set forth at a steady but more cautious pace.

Not that one had to go far to hear what the townsfolk had to say. The air buzzed with stories. One man suspected a business partner of stealing. Another had trouble with trench foot. A third had written his sweetheart asking for her to wait for him.

Murmured hopes. Gruff complaints. She knew them well.

If Cormac knew only a quarter of the hellholes she'd been in, he'd look at her differently. The gun in her pocket was his first glimpse into the depths of her less-than-ladylike character. Her descent had started long ago during the war. Despite warning Declan not to join the war effort too young, she'd swiftly followed suit. Back then, she'd wanted to be invisible. And she had. No one had paid attention to her dressed in the rags of a teenage boy. But she'd paid attention to everyone and everything around her. She'd always been good at listening. Knowing what to do with what she'd heard had followed naturally.

"They're stealing our farms." The statement came from inside a tall tent.

Adella halted, senses on full alert. Cormac had mentioned troubles with farmers. Could the person in the tent be one of them?

She didn't recognize the woman's voice, but she recognized the sentiment in it. Words uttered halting, thick with tears, its owner struggling to deal with a seemingly irresolvable calamity. The voice was also thick with an accent from the old world. The r's rolled, the t's pronounced like d's, suggesting not England or even Scotland, but a land further north. Sweden or possibly Norway.

"Stealing? The railroad's paying you, surely? There must be a misunderstanding." This voice Adella knew. Kate Parsons.

Keeping her footsteps soft, Adella hastened to the tent's opening, a flap tied back to form an inverted V large enough to peek through but still keep oneself hidden. Inside, the light was dim, but Kate's vibrant red hair was unmistakable. She sat on a bench facing a raised stage. Two clusters of women—dressed in crisp, Sunday-best bonnets and frayed, everyday jackets of homespun wool—huddled on either side of her. Like hens round a fox, they darted glances at Kate.

On the stage, a pair of black-garbed missionaries, somber and silent as gravestones, flanked a life-size cross. Before them paced a woman with hair so blonde it appeared white. She had a long, rolling stride—heavy and noisy as a man's—and the robust frame of an Amazon matriarch. She could probably drive a plow team all morning, plant the field that afternoon, and tackle a dozen other laborious chores before bedtime.

"If there's a misunderstanding," the blonde woman replied in the accent that had first snagged Adella's attention, "it's yours and your father's."

"Helga!" gasped a woman seated near Kate. "Shouldn't we give our guest the benefit of the doubt? With our husbands killed in the war and our farms failing—" She turned to Kate and bowing her head murmured, "We have so very little, Miss Parsons, and you and your father have so much. Surely, as your father, he holds your opinion in great regard. You will help us, won't you?"

"I will talk to my father." With her head held high, Kate stood to leave.

Adella ducked out of sight behind the tent. Kate's footsteps tapped a determined beat on the wooden path before fading away.

"We need more than talk," Helga grumbled inside the tent. "I've asked the Lord a hundred times for help. But He let the war take my Wilhelm. Now He's letting the railroad take the one thing Wilhelm left me."

The silence that followed allowed even a horse, whining faintly in the distance, to be heard. The sun's warmth brushed Adella's back. God helped those who helped themselves, and this opportunity was ripe with possibilities—for both her and the farm widows.

Lifting the flap, she let the light spill around her. It illuminated the base of the cross. She pushed the opening wider, so the beam travelled up to fully gild God's reminder of his son's victory over sin and death. Everyone twisted round to stare in her direction, just as she'd hoped.

"Who's there?" Helga asked, squinting.

Strolling up the aisle, so they'd now see more than her dark silhouette, Adella smiled at each woman she passed as if she were greeting old friends at a church social. "My name is Adella Willows. I work for a newspaper out East."

Helga folded her arms. "Never had use for reading outside the Bible."

Adella sat in Kate's vacated seat, propping her camera before her to draw attention to the device. "I was exploring the town for a story to photograph when—" she forced the frown that came naturally to her brow to deepen for effect, "—I overheard your plight. I sympathize with your struggle, as I've seen many suffer similarly during my work."

Helga snorted. "You and your fancy pictures can't do us a lick of good."

Adella met Helga's glare without blinking. "If a subject is powerful, then so is the photograph."

"Can pictures stop the railroad from taking our land?"

"They've helped similar causes." Adella gestured to her valise. "If you have time, I could show you." Without waiting for an answer, she set her bag on the stage and opened it.

Her fingers skimmed the top of a closed compartment. Drawing determination from the letters concealed there, she leafed through the photographs and newspaper clippings in plain sight. Behind her, the benches squeaked as her audience rose and edged closer. She spread several items in front of the cross.

"Here are the women-led labor strikes." She pointed to each story as she spoke. "Lowell Mills in the 30s and 40s, the New England Shoemakers in 1860, and the Collar Laundry Union just last year. All protests organized by women seeking social justice like improved wages and working conditions."

The women stared at the pictures in silence. Weavers and cobblers and laundresses were all fine and dandy, but this audience needed something a little closer to home. Adella extracted an engraved poster from her valise.

"What's that?" Helga asked.

"A promotional poster for the Grange Movement. They encourage farm families to band together for the well-being of their community, including uniting against unfair practices by railroads."

Helga finally drew near and bent to scan the poster. "They're taking on the railroads?"

"Protest rallies have proved effective. Peacefully obstructing a worksite can not only create disruptions, but great pictures that sell newspapers and sway public opinion. The Katy's in a race with a rival railroad to win thousands of acres of land. Time is worth more to them than the few acres that make up your farms. They just need to be reminded of that fact."

"Then what're we waiting for? When the sun's shining and the snow's melting, you don't sit by the window and contemplate the view." Helga may not have been an avid reader outside of the Bible but, as every farmer worth her salt, she grasped the importance of time. She also grasped Adella by the elbow and said, "We're going to the worksite and making the railroad feel our loss right now."

The suddenness of Helga's grasp combined with the fact that the woman deemed it necessary to grab hold of her at all, made Adella's stomach lurch. She squelched her unease. Helga was just...enthusiastic. She wasn't Adella's enemy. They shared similar goals. And standing in a missionary tent surrounded by women—especially one who championed your cause with Viking determination and swiftness—hardly classified as a dangerous situation.

"My buckboard's outside." Helga lifted Adella's camera with one hand and propelled her forward with the other.

She barely had time to grab her valise and her pictures. With the women close behind, they exited the tent only stopping beside a wagon harnessed to a pair of swayback nags.

"Get in," Helga instructed, releasing Adella. Then she climbed onto the driver's seat and set the camera beside her.

Adella offered each woman encouragement and a helping hand as they clambered aboard. When everyone was settled, she hopped up to perch on the open tailgate with her valise on her lap and her feet dangling over the mud. Helga snapped the reins and the wagon rolled forward.

The women started singing. "*Ye Christian Heroes, Wake to Glory. Hark, hark! What millions bid you rise!*" When the hymn ended, they promptly began another. They'd just completed a poignant rendition of the old favorite *Onward Christian Soldiers* when the horses slowed to pick their way over a swath of freshly overturned earth slanting down to a mangled gully.

Was this the ravine that the McGrady Gang had mentioned dynamiting into submission?

Adella's heart beat faster. Hopefully they

wouldn't be putting themselves in further danger today. She shook her head. She shouldn't be thinking about Cormac and his men's safety. She should be thinking about Declan and her mission. The worksite couldn't be far ahead. What would Cormac do when she and the women arrived? Whatever he did, she must soldier on and outwit him.

The women kept singing, only stopping when Helga said, "There's the camp."

Directly ahead, stood a tent with empty tables and benches at one end and steaming pots tended by a handful of men at the other. None of the men came close to rivaling Cormac's giant form. Adella's gaze kept moving, searching.

Not far beyond the chow tent, Stevens' railcar slumbered silently on freshly laid track. Farther ahead, the rest of the train vibrated under half steam with a flurry of men milling around its front. Several workers stood on its freight car, carefully sliding down a ramp one of the hefty rails that had nearly crushed her yesterday. On the ground, a row of men lifted the rail using oversized tongs and lugged it the short distance ahead of the engine. Releasing their burden, they retraced their steps to the stockcar, leaving room for a third group who swung their hammers and nailed the rail into its final resting place.

Meanwhile the rail's partner had already coasted down the ramp and was being carried forward.

The men labored without their leader. That didn't surprise her. They were so well organized they didn't need Cormac. The rare combination of an assembly line designed for speed while still striving to make the labor as easy as possible for each worker suggested Cormac's handiwork. She'd only known him a day, but she was already attuned to his concerned pragmatism. A trait that pleased then irked her. She had no desire to like anything about him. And she was only hunting for him so he would not sneak up on her unnoticed again.

The only other men in sight were those who groomed a band of earth that became increasingly disheveled until it disappeared over a rise. That presumably was where the cut crew would be. The McGrady Gang and possibly Cormac as well. All working. Swiftly. Productively. Without delay.

How could men function so well after consuming so much alcohol the night before?

Despite all her scheming, she felt slow-witted to imagine she could've laid them low with that old trick. *Blasted Irish.*

The wagon had drawn even with the chow tent. The scent of the noon meal, boiling potatoes and pork roasting on spits, curled around her. Pausing their preparations, the cooks returned the women's stares.

"What do we do now?" one of the farm widows whispered.

"We assemble on the track and stop construction."

A smile tugged at Adella's lips. Helga had things well in hand.

"Then we get our picture taken and go home," Helga added.

Adella's contentment vanished along with her smile. She needed them to delay construction as long as possible. If a picture would make them leave, then she couldn't take it. She needed to disappear without the women noticing. For that she needed a distraction.

"Why not educate these lost souls using the gift God gave you—your voices raised together in song?" she asked.

Once more the women launched into a hymn. The chow gang dropped their ladles and cleavers and followed the wagon. Up ahead, the clanging and scraping stopped, replaced by the thump of approaching footsteps. Soon the wagon was swarmed by a ring of gawking men. With a firm hand on the reins, Helga forged a path through them while the other women stared stoically forward and continued singing.

Adella scanned the rise again. It remained blessedly empty. It wouldn't for long. Resigned to the fact that she must temporarily abandon her camera, she tightened her grip on her valise and slipped off the wagon into the crowd. The women didn't notice, but the men did. Luckily, they didn't comment and only gaped at her as she pushed by them. Their attention soon returned to the noisy wagon.

"The chief ain't gonna have nothin' good to say about this." This observation came from her left. Weaving her way through the crowd in that direction, she spied two youths slouching against Stevens' private railcar while they observed the passing parade.

She ducked behind the rear of the car and held her breath.

"But he won't be sayin' it till he returns with the surveyors. Plenty of time fer a closer look."

"The chief said we couldn't leave our post."

"You worry too much about what ol' prissy pants Stevens says. He ain't gonna know we left."

"But he said—"

"Fine. You stay behind."

Peeking around the railcar, Adella watched the pair—one leading, the other following—jog after the wagon. She climbed the steps at the rear of Stevens' railcar. What a shame he wouldn't be in to receive her.

The door opened easily under her hand. She crept down a narrow oak-paneled hall past a door fitted into the inner wall. It most likely led to Stevens' bedchamber. The velvet curtain at the end of the hall intrigued her more. Slipping through it, she found his office.

The same oak from the hall circled the room, not only muffling the sound of travel but the voices outside. Interspersed with the thick brocade shades, conveniently pulled down to conceal her, the snug room felt like a hushed forest. It made the click of her boots overly loud as she took the two steps required to stand beside a desk grand enough for a king.

She set her valise on the floor and got to work. Out of habit, she kept her search tidy, returning items to their place so no one would know she'd been there. She counseled herself against expecting to find anything. Stevens wasn't a fool. He wouldn't leave anything he deemed incriminating lying about. Nevertheless, she scanned the mundane with the same vigor as she'd give a signed confession of guilt.

The telegram paper was parchment thin, the writing on it just as sparse. But the information it contained was weighty and made her heart race.

Men grumbling.
Wage increased to 3 dollars and 50 cents.
Laid more track than any day last week.
Arrival moved up.

She retrieved the account book she'd discovered earlier in a drawer. Flipping to the last page with writing, she traced her index finger down the rows. The thrill of discovery shot through her, halting her hand.

Laborers' wages...$3.00 a day.

The telegram wasn't a report on the Katy's progress but the Joy Line's. Stevens had his spies as well. She'd have to keep a careful lookout for them...and Joy's man who dumped the load yesterday and nearly crushed her. Dangers abounded, but after the war she'd grown used to most of them. What frightened her most was failing Declan. Again.

She forced herself to exhale a deep, calming breath. Right now the important thing was the difference of half a dollar. In her hands rested the beginnings of a wage war. She folded the paper twice and tucked it in her cleavage.

Across the office, footfalls scraped the steps behind the second door, accompanied by a muffled voice growing louder. She thrust the account book back in its drawer and ducked through the thick fall of drapery into the hall.

Her adrenaline deserted her in a whoosh, making her sag against the wall. She pressed her palms over her stomach to steady herself—then raised her hands before her eyes in horror. They were both empty! Spinning round, she glimpsed through the crack in the curtain her valise on the floor beside Stevens' desk. Behind it, the door banged open to reveal Stevens himself.

She jerked back.

"Inside," Stevens barked. "I refuse to have this conversation out where everyone can hear." Swift footsteps stomped across the room, making Adella's pulse roar in her ears like a freight train was approaching. The chair behind Stevens' desk squeaked, and the pounding in her head vanished.

"I want those goddamn women off my track."

The only response to Stevens' demand was the door clicking softly shut.

Edging forward, she peeked through the curtain. Stevens sat with his back to her, facing a man standing on the other side of his desk. She wasn't surprised to see it was

Cormac. His quietness had given him away.

Her valise wasn't in Stevens' line of sight, but it was within Cormac's. He just needed to turn his head a little to the left. Fortunately, his gaze was locked on Stevens. Unfortunately, her escape hung on his attention staying there.

Perspiration trickled down between her breasts, jerking her attention back to the need to escape with the telegram. Retrieving her valise was more important. Its contents were her only link to the past, to all those who'd struggled and suffered—including Declan. Abandoning his letters would be like abandoning him.

"Give those widows a reason and they'll go willingly," Cormac said. "Give them back their farms."

She felt her jaw drop. Why was she surprised? Cormac had championed his men and her. Why not others? But how did he think he could build a railroad for men like Parsons and Stevens, and still treat people fairly?

Stevens flicked his hand. "Not an option."

"Is that why you didn't tell me about them earlier?" The challenging note, the one Cormac used with Stevens yesterday at the station, had returned. "Everything along this railroad is yours to give. Or take."

"Careful, McGrady." Stevens' voice was as chilled as frozen ditchwater. "If you don't order the men to remove those women, I can take your job."

"I won't hurt innocent women."

"They aren't innocent." Stevens' fist slammed the desktop. "They're on my track illegally. And if track isn't laid, you don't get paid."

Cormac folded his arms over his chest. "Better that than manhandling a woman."

"You realize the men won't be paid either." Stevens' voice had gone deceptively calm. She knew the tone. She'd heard it during the war whenever an ambitious captain believed he'd found the key to squeezing one more cavalry charge out of his men.

The muscles across Cormac's shoulders tensed. He spun away from Stevens, as if he couldn't stand the sight of him. He ended up staring straight at her valise.

Her stomach did a slow, sickly roll.

Cormac remained stiff and silent for a long time. Then he snarled something in Gaelic.

Stevens huffed out a breath. "What the hell does that mean? Speak English, man."

"I've been blind to too many things."

"I don't care if you're blind, deaf and dumb, as long as you do your job."

Cormac headed toward the door. "You

should try talking to the widows one more time while I fetch the photographer."

Stevens leapt to his feet. "For Chrissake! A picture of this debacle is the last thing we need."

"The farmers' leader, the blonde woman, said they weren't leaving until they had their photograph taken." Cormac halted by the door. "What's more important continuing construction or one photograph that might never see the light of day?"

Stevens lowered his chin. He glared at the papers on his desk for a long moment. "You guarantee the picture will disappear?"

"I do."

"No need for an audience, the widows, or the men. Destroy the picture while escorting Miss Willows and her camera back to town. Make sure she gets there. I've had enough of women pestering me."

Cormac nodded slowly. "Miss Willows will do what's best for the safety of all those concerned."

"What happens if these widows return tomorrow and pull the same stunt?" Stevens grumbled, retracing his steps to the door.

Cormac opened it for him. The faint strains of a hymn drifted in. "Give them back their homes or pay them fairly. Can't see any other choices." He dipped his head in a mock bow, waiting for Stevens to precede him outside. "But I'm just the foreman. You're the chief."

As soon as the door clicked shut, Adella leapt through the curtain and grabbed her valise. Then she darted back to her hiding place. She didn't go any further though. And she wasn't surprised when, after the count of twenty, the door opened and closed softly again.

"Now that you've retrieved your case," Cormac said, "we can fetch your camera."

She stepped out from behind the curtain, scouring her mind for another delay. Her wits failed her under his piercing silver gaze, until she blurted, "We'll have to go to town. I left my camera in my hotel room."

"Your camera's in the widows' wagon. Luckily Stevens hasn't seen it. Yet." He squeezed shut his eyes and pressed his fingertips to his eyelids. "Do you even know how to operate the device or is that a sham as well?"

"Of course I know how," Adella said, forcing outrage into her voice. "I'm a photographer sent by the *Atlanta Intelligencer.*"

Cormac snorted. "If that were true, you'd be with the widows instead of in here. There's only one reason for being in Stevens' railcar—you're a spy for the Joy Line." He grasped her elbow, making her skin tingle as he pushed her in front of him toward the door. He tucked her behind him, though, when he stuck his head outside.

Pressed against the warm strength of his back, she tried to block out the anger vibrating in him. But the singing reminded her that her next move would probably make him even angrier.

He pulled her down the stairs toward the women. "I wondered why you'd come to New Chicago. I could never have guessed this."

"Then be prepared for even greater disappointments." She dug her heels into the soft dirt. "What if I refuse to act out this useless charade of taking a picture that will—how did you put it?—*never see the light of day?*"

Swinging round, he bent over her. "Adella, if you don't cooperate, I can't protect those women or you."

A peculiar ache invaded her heart. What would it feel like to share her burdens with someone like Cormac instead of shouldering them alone? She wouldn't be sharing; she'd be giving up. Declan deserved more than that. She yearned to wrap her arms around Cormac and pull him even closer. So she drew back instead. "By all means save the widows. But I don't need help."

His arm snaked around her waist, halting her retreat. "Judging how you end up in places you shouldn't, I don't think you give a tinker's damn about your own well-being."

Keeping a firm grip on her valise, she wedged her other hand between them. Against her palm, his heart raced in time with her own.

"You're taking those women's picture so everyone can go safely home."

"Soon they won't have a home to go to," she shot back.

"But they'll be alive. I haven't time to argue with you. Those women—"

"Have every right to—"

"They're in danger the moment the men realize who's responsible for them not getting paid."

Unease prickled the nerves along her neck. "The men? Surely the McGrady Gang wouldn't—"

"Not them. The others."

The draft of a memory stole over her, transporting her back to last night. She shivered. "The three men outside Eden's."

He nodded. "Them and others like them."

"You employ thugs?" she said, trying to sound shocked. But she was already well acquainted with men of the sort. Men who justified their actions, committed unthinkable atrocities, and destroyed their own souls in the process. She'd learned too much about them during Sherman's sacking of the south.

"I hired anyone who came looking for work. The only ones I'll vouch for are the McGrady Gang." His hold on her waist tightened and his eyes narrowed, pinning her with a sudden intensity. "You keep that in mind wherever you are. If you're in danger, come get me. If you can't find me, go to the McGrady Gang. Never any of the others."

"I don't need—"

He gave her a tiny shake. "*Never* trust any of the others. You hear me?"

"I'm just a newspaper photographer. Little danger in that." That argument sounded weak, even to her ears. So did her voice.

"Adella...stop playing games. Promise. Swear on whatever you hold dear. I don't care about the rest. I won't let anyone else die because of me."

The utter pain etched on his face made her gasp. "Who—?"

He released her, his expression turning blank and distant. "Just do this one thing. Promise you'll come to me if you're in danger."

She swallowed the urge to do as he requested, if only to ease whatever burdened him. "I can't promise you anything," she whispered. "You work for my enemy."

Standing beside Cormac, Adella watched the women climb back onto Helga's wagon. The farm widows chattered happily. Even the missionaries couldn't suppress their smiles. Worry and guilt sat heavily on Adella's shoulders. She shouldn't have revealed that Cormac worked for her enemy, and she shouldn't have promised the widows a photograph she now couldn't deliver. She'd taken their picture posing in front of the train, but soon Cormac would destroy the photographic plate and there'd be no story for any newspaper.

She glanced at Cormac. With her camera under one arm, he stared at the women, his shoulders hunched as if the weight of the present and past bothered him as well. Who had died to cause him such pain and…remorse? She struggled to suppress her concern for him. He might not be pondering what he'd let slip. He might be calculating where on the trail to town to turn his attention to her camera and smash the plate.

He works for your enemy, she reminded herself, and he takes his work as seriously as you do.

She thrust her hand in the air. "Helga, wait! I want…"

Helga and the women fell silent, waiting

with raised eyebrows for her to continue.

She stepped forward. "I want to ride back with—"

Cormac's hand clamped down on her shoulder. "What Miss Willows wants to say is that she'd *like* to ride with you, but she's promised to ride with me."

Adella tried to twist free of his grasp. "I promised you nothing," she hissed under her breath. "They need this photograph."

He turned her away from the women. "If Miss Willows wishes, she can visit your farms tomorrow. More photographs can be taken then." He nudged her toward the chow tent. As soon as they were out of earshot, he muttered, "Why must you be so stubborn? You know you can't go with them. You heard me promise Stevens I'd escort you back to town."

"I heard you argue with him too." She squirmed under his hand. This time he let her go. "You told him to give the widows their due." She studied Cormac from of the corner of her eye. "Why didn't you tell Stevens I was in his railcar?"

Cormac lengthened his stride, leaving her to follow. Behind the chow tent, a row of horses stood tied to a line. They lifted their dozing heads, snorting in surprise and pricking their ears forward.

"Can you ride?" he asked.

"Of course." She bit back the reminder

that her father had been a horse trainer. Irritated that Cormac had so easily avoided her question with one of his own, she scowled at him and made a sweeping gesture along her dress. "But I couldn't possibly ride astride in a dress this fitted."

"Then why wear it?"

Because the dress is doing its job. Again. If she couldn't ride into town—for whatever reason, then Cormac couldn't resume his work. Every minute she spent delaying his efforts to escort her back to New Chicago could coincide with a breakdown in construction that he'd be too busy to fix. She must keep him with her as long as possible. She straightened her shoulders, gathering her resolve. There was a silver lining to this setback.

So why hadn't she thought to stay by his side sooner rather than trying to leave with the women? Because she was a spy, a deceiver, and a thief—although he hadn't discovered this last part yet—and she didn't want to hear how much of a disappointment she was to him. Unfortunately, that was sure to happen if he hung around her long enough. But so far he'd said little on the subject. Instead, he'd talked of her safety and the women's. And right now he continued staring at her, demanding answers to questions she couldn't answer truthfully.

"I wear the dress because it's pretty."

He cupped her cheek, making her skin flame under his hand. "You'd make my oldest shirt look breathtaking."

The prospect of standing before him wearing one of his linen shirts, and only that, made her face burn even hotter. His gaze searched hers, while his thumb caressed her cheekbone. Her heart raced in her chest. He tugged her closer. She didn't stop him.

Maybe her dress was doing its job a little too well. Could she use seduction to keep Cormac from his work? She'd never gone that far in all her years as a spy. But then she'd never been this attracted to a man before.

"I'm not your enemy," he whispered. "I want to know you better. There are a hundred things I want to ask...starting with why you consider Stevens to be yours."

Her lips parted in surprise. "Stevens?"

"You said I worked for your enemy."

An unfortunate slip, that. But while Cormac was busy concentrating on Stevens, he wouldn't be rooting out her real target. Besides, all of Parsons' employees were by default her enemies. Their livelihoods would suffer significant setbacks when she financially ruined Parsons. Cormac and the McGrady Gang didn't deserve that. Remorse made her bow her head.

"What happened to your brother?" Cormac asked.

His question hit her like a slap to the face. It took all of her resolve not to flinch. She wasn't sure she succeeded. So she summoned a lie in the hopes of distracting him. "He died, and I hadn't thought of him for years, not until I saw Fergal."

"You can tell me the truth."

"I am," she snapped.

"I won't tell Stevens that you were in his railcar. I won't tell him any of your secrets."

She pulled away from him and clutched her valise against her stomach. "Don't say things you'll regret later. Like promises you can't keep."

"I'll protect you. I won't see you hurt." His voice was firm and resolute.

"Why? Because of *your* past? Who died because of you?"

He stared at her with wide eyes.

She immediately regretted her bluntness. She'd allowed her unsettling attraction to Cormac to not only make her foolish but shrewish. "I shouldn't have asked that. I'm sorry."

His gaze slid away from her, unfocused and distant. Then he shook his head as if dispelling ghosts. "You're the most confusing woman I ever met." He raked his free hand through his hair.

She wished she could do the same, but in

a more soothing gesture.

"But I've promised to protect you and I will," he said. "I've also promised to return you to town, which aids my first promise." He handed back her camera, then unlashed a barrel from a small table that turned out to have wheels instead of legs.

"What's that?" she asked.

"A wagon." He rolled the barrel onto the ground.

She blinked, trying to reconcile the word with the object before her. All she saw was a three-foot square of wood supported between two wheels. "Looks more like a dog cart."

"We use it to transport water to the men." Cormac tied her camera where the barrel had been, leaving room in front. Then he chose a horse from the line and backed it into the traces of his so-called wagon. Speaking softly in Gaelic, he harnessed the fidgety mare with swift movements that spoke of a familiarity with such tasks.

He was a little more abrupt with her when he grabbed her round the waist and plopped her before her camera on the cart. The contraption wobbled horribly, the weathered wood creaking. It reminded her of New Chicago's ramshackle train station.

"I wager we'll part company with a wheel before we're even halfway to town." She suppressed a smile.

Cormac stared at her for a long moment. Then he climbed up beside her. His thigh settled against hers, solid and unmovable, and inappropriately intimate. He didn't move away and give her space, although if he'd tried, their narrow seat might not have allowed it. He didn't try.

Her heart was now pounding so fast she thought it might leap out her throat. Setting her valise on her lap, she busied herself smoothing her skirt around her ankles.

He clicked his tongue and the cart rocked into motion. "I can handle a lost wheel. But if you slip off this wagon and try to disappear like you did with the farm widows, I'll carry you into town over my shoulder and ask the authorities to toss you in jail for... For disturbing the peace. God knows, you've certainly disturbed mine."

Chapter 5

Cormac hoped Adella wouldn't see through his bluff. He couldn't throw her in jail. If someone questioned her and discovered why she'd come to town, she might not make it out alive. He'd heard too many times about frontier justice acting swift and burying their mistakes in the dark of the night.

Adella was playing a dangerous game, but she hadn't hurt anyone. He frowned. At least not anyone he knew of. He shook his head to cast out his doubts. Adella wasn't like the man who'd been sabotaging the railroad. That man had almost killed her.

But she was still a spy. He had two spies to deal with now. And if two, then why not three? Or four? Or more? The thought was daunting. Not as daunting as knowing what to do with the woman sitting next to him though.

He allowed himself a slow soft curse, in

Gaelic so she wouldn't know what he said. Building a railroad was challenging enough without half-wild workers, protesting farm widows, and a spy who he was more attracted to than any woman he'd ever met. He must use the half-hour it would take to travel to town wisely. He must figure out the conundrum Adella Willows represented.

Unfortunately, the woman sitting next to him was damnably distracting. She perched beside him with her thigh rubbing his. She kept readjusting her skirt, her movements amplifying his already heightened awareness of her. He'd never met anyone more alive. Why did a bright young woman like this choose such a dangerous profession?

"How much is the Joy Line paying you?" he asked.

Her jaw tightened. "I'm getting what I need."

The cart lurched and he tore his gaze from her. They'd reached the ravine his men had filled yesterday. The ground on either side of the track was a slick slope. He angled the cart for the track. The rickety thing would be better off travelling over the rails than through the mud. He decided this too late, and when the mare was on the track, the cart remained stuck in the mud.

"Whoa, now. Steady, girl." The mare ignored him and continued pulling.

Keeping a firm hand on the reins, he jumped to the ground, putting himself between Adella and the closest slope. "Best get down, lass. Hop off the other side of the wagon and onto the tracks. Then I'll push the cart out." He widened his stance, bracing his toe against the wheel and his palm against the seat. "I've plenty of experience from the bogs 'round Galway."

"I'm even more familiar. An Irish bog is no match for a Georgia swamp." With her valise clutched on her lap, Adella shimmied across the wagon seat toward him. She held out her free hand. "Give me the reins."

He drew them out of her reach. The mare tossed her head, rattling her bridle. Then she lunged. The cart emitted a startling crack and tipped, sliding Adella even closer to him.

Releasing the cart, he raised a cautionary hand between them. "Keep still. The wheel's coming loose. If it does, I can't stop you from falling in the mud. Whatever you are, you're still a lady. I don't think you want to get dirty again or walk all the way to town."

"And I don't think you know me very well, Mr. McGrady." She lifted her skirt giving him a tantalizing view of her legs from trim ankle to shapely knee, making his heart race. She lifted one dainty foot.

His heart skipped a beat. "Adella,

don't—"

She stomped her heel on top of the wheel. Pain exploded in his shin as the wheel came free. Without its support the cart collapsed, sending Adella crashing into his chest, toppling him backward.

He released the reins. He wouldn't drag the horse down with them and cause it injury. Instead, his hands instinctively wrapped around Adella's waist. They fell together—her on top, his back taking the brunt of the impact—and slid down the ravine. The horse whinnied and whatever was left of the cart rattled off along the track.

Their descent halted as abruptly as it began. Cormac lay motionless with his eyes squeezed shut, laboring to draw in a full breath. When he did, his discomfort vanished. He became intensely aware of Adella's legs against his. Under his palms, her torso was silky smooth, but something hard poked him in the chest. Something *between* him and Adella. He cracked one eye open.

She'd managed to keep that damnable bag with her. The one she'd rather hold onto than accept his hand at the train station. The one she'd rather risk capture than leave in Stevens' railcar.

"Are you all right?" She stared down at him with wide amber eyes. So close. Not close enough.

He could only grunt a yes.

She released a breath, almost like she'd been holding it. "I suspect otherwise. No doubt, you feel you must act all stoic and manly. I'm sorry if I caused you injury and I regret my...enthusiasm. Perhaps I should not have kicked the wheel quite so hard." She folded her hands on top of the bag and rested her chin on them, her expression unreadable—as if she regretted nothing, as if she weren't affected by their sudden intimacy.

Frustration rolled through him like thunder after a flash of lightning. She did not blink as she watched him. Nor did she have the good grace to meet his gaze again. Instead, she stared at a point somewhere between his nose and chin. The delicate flick of her tongue across her lips sent him over the edge.

He wrenched the bag out from between them and flung it as far as he could. Pushing up on her elbows, she tracked it with wide eyes as it bounced out of reach.

"Go on," he growled. "Go after you precious bag." His traitorous hands returned to her waist, countermanding his order. "At the worksite you abandoned your camera. Now you don't even look where it might have gone. But that bag? You care more about it than your own safety."

Her gaze returned to him, narrowing. "You become testy over the oddest things. Are you sure you are uninjured?"

"I'm fine. But you need to get up. I'm taking you to town."

"Why not toss me after my valise and return to your precious railroad?"

"Because I don't manhandle women, no matter how..." he ground his teeth, "...frustrating they are. Nor do I abandon them on the prairie where anything could happen to them. Not even when they are foolhardy and duplicitous. Now get up. We're going to town."

She didn't move, just continued staring at him. "You didn't think it could get any worse than me being English. Well, I'm a lot worse. Sorry to disappoint."

"My only disappointment is that you kicked the wheel off our cart."

"It was bound to come off sooner or later. I just hurried along the inevitable."

"This day couldn't get any poorer." He pressed his lips tight to control another petty outburst.

Her shoulders sagged and she slumped against him as if wounded by his words. Her bosom settled soft against his chest, her pelvis snug over his. She drew back her head. But the rest of her stayed where it was. "Mr. McGrady...Cormac." Her voice was a throaty purr. His name swirled like a lover's caress around his ear.

If he thought having her legs touching his was distracting, it was nothing to having her entire body—minus her bag—stretched out full length on top of him.

He immediately released her waist. "You're—" His throat closed up and he cleared it roughly. "You're in a very compromising situation. I suggest you move for that reason alone. Or do you always seduce men to get what you want?"

"Right now, I don't know what I want."

He swallowed hard. "Adella, don't play games with me."

"I'm not playing at anything." Gaze locked on his mouth, she lowered her head. "I'm…"

She kept leaning closer. All he could do was stare at her. At her lips. Plump and pink and parted. Damn the consequences. He was going to kiss her.

A soft nicker sounded nearby. Adella glanced toward the noise. The mare had wandered down the slope and stood a handful of strides away.

Adella's gaze found his again. "I'm an idiot to let you distract me so completely. I hadn't even noticed that blasted cart was still around." Adella's muscles tensed, preparing for action.

"Adella, don't," he said, reaching for her again.

Her knees and elbows suddenly poked him in too many sensitive places. As slippery as a bar of soap, she escaped him and crawled through the mud. So much for assuming she cared about getting dirty.

He scrambled after her. His fingers snared her skirt. Too late. She waved her hands in the horse's face, shooing it away. The cart cracked in two. The camera, rope still tangled around it, fell toward the mud. With a gasp, she dove to catch it.

His hold on her skirt brought her up short. The camera hit the mud with a splash and the mare galloped toward town, probably heading for an oat bucket in the livery.

Adella glared over her shoulder at him.

"I hope your camera isn't broken." He released her skirt, raising his hand to rake it through his hair. He stopped when he saw the mud covering his fingers. "But if it is, it's your own doing. And what for? All you've accomplished is that rather than riding into town, we're walking."

She turned her profile to him and the furrow lines on her brow slowly smoothed out, retreating behind an impenetrable mask. She retrieved her camera and valise, and sat down crossed legged with them on her lap.

"What are you doing?" Climbing to his feet, he moved to stand in front of her. "I'm escorting you back to town."

Once more, she folded her hands over her bag. But this time fixed her gaze on the empty horizon. "You can't force me to walk beside you."

The way she'd phrased her words, made his insides hollow. "Who said anything about you walking?"

After a barrage of cursing and thumping Cormac's back with her valise and her free hand, Adella settled into a tight-lipped silence. Hanging over his shoulder, she watched her camera rock in a sling he'd fashioned from rope.

Why hadn't she thought of a carrier like that? Damn him for being so handy, and her for being so reckless. Her impetuous acts had broken the plate but luckily not her camera. She couldn't rail at Cormac for the loss of the farm widows' photograph. She had only herself to blame.

Keeping an arm behind her knees, he held her prisoner and strode toward town at an annoyingly effortless pace. Each step caused her head to bob. His shoulder dug uncomfortably into her belly. The back of her throat burned.

"You must grow tired of carrying me," she said.

"I'm fine."

"Why not—" Her voice sounded odd, thready and stifled. She tried again. "Why not put me down and save your back?"

"My back's fine, too."

A sickly heat washed over her and her vision blurred. "I'm eager to walk." The declaration burst from her lips, rising alarmingly on the last word.

"I'm eager to reach town."

"Cormac, I—"

"No."

"Please," she managed on the back of a groan. "Put me down."

He immediately set her on her feet. She felt like a child's top with the string yanked free. The sky, and Cormac looming high above her, spun in a blur of grays and browns.

"What's wrong?" His voice sounded far away.

"I feel—" She drew in a shuddery breath, willing her breakfast to stay in place. "I feel—" She gulped again.

"You look seasick. Lean forward with your hands on your knees." His hand on her neck, gentle but firm, forced her to comply. "Why didn't you say something sooner?"

She shook her head. Her gut heaved, freezing her into stillness. "I could not."

"Stubborn English."

"Opinionated Irish," she shot back, then groaned again.

Slowly her stomach settled. She became aware of his work-roughened fingers massaging her neck with infinite tenderness. How long had he been doing that? She raised her head and straightened her back, so she could look him in the face.

He kept his hand around the nape of her neck. "Better now?"

Gaze riveted on his face, she swayed toward him. She only did so, she told herself, because it might aid her mission, not because she wanted him to continue touching her. "I can't go to jail."

He released her abruptly and stepped back. "I told you not to play games with me, lass."

"But—"

"I'm not putting you in jail."

"But you said if I misbehaved, you'd carry me over your shoulder and—"

"I don't know what to do with you, but I know a jail cell won't help." Muttering the now familiar Gaelic curse, he grasped her hand and tugged her forward. "We still need to get to town and moving will help take your mind off things."

Laced with hers, his fingers were warm and reassuring. She didn't want to argue with him. He might let go. But she had to delay his return to the worksite.

As if sensing her thoughts, his grip tightened. "Stop plotting your next move. If your mind, or your stomach, won't settle, then pick a point on the horizon and concentrate on taking slow, even breaths."

"Aye, aye. Captain," she muttered and did as he said.

They walked for several minutes in silence, before he finally chuckled. "I can't believe you chased off our horse. Or kicked off that wheel."

Another long silence passed, filled only with sound of their strides swishing through the grass.

"What made you become a spy?" His voice was quiet, lacking any merriment.

The answer filled her mind but didn't touch her lips: *Declan.*

Fearless and protective, her brother had insisted she accompany him on all his childhood campaigns. Then he'd abandoned her and signed up with Fergal to fight a war she'd never understood. Since that day, she hadn't willingly spoken his name. How could she when her other half—her twin, her constant companion, her best friend for fifteen years—was gone? Taken from her, first by his own familiar hand, then forever by the cold, pitiless hands of strangers?

She might not say Declan's name, but he was never far from invading her thoughts. He was the gaping hole in her soul, the wound that would not heal.

Sudden tears blurred her vision. She

turned away from Cormac and rubbed her brow, hiding behind her hand...her empty hand. A sensation ten times more horrible than being sick to her stomach engulfed her. She spun round and searched the path they'd just travelled.

"I've lost my valise!" She tried to sprint back down the path.

Cormac held her fast. "Adella, it's all right. I have your bag." He held it up for her to see.

Her spine sagged with relief. "How long have you had it?"

"Since I set you on the ground and you dropped it."

"But...why carry it for me? When we fell in the mud, you cursed it and threw it away."

"It's important to you, so I couldn't leave it behind." He stared at the ground between them. "I only did so, because I didn't want you running back for it and further delaying our trip."

"I can take it now." She held out her hand.

He put his body between her and her goal. "Why's it so important to you?"

Best not to tell him about the photographs and newspaper clippings inside. Or Declan's letters. Cormac already knew too much.

She forced herself to drop her hand to

her side. "I've owned the valise a long time. It's merely a sentimental attachment."

"Then you won't mind me continuing to carry it for you." He started walking again and she followed suit.

She didn't really have a choice, she told herself. He was still holding her hand. She aimed for the lethargic stride of a woman resigned to defeat, which wasn't hard. He'd won the battle. She couldn't stop him from reaching town. Like the wheel coming off the cart, she could only control the speed of which the inevitable happened. She considered him out of the corner of her eye. Only, she told herself, to ensure he continued to carry her valise.

Whistling an Irish ditty under his breath, he walked beside her without a word or glance to chastise her slowness. They were both dirty up to the knee, but his entire back was caked in mud. He'd taken the brunt of their fall and his protectiveness continued. When she stumbled over a rock, his hand tightened reassuringly around hers. When she paused to pluck a pebble from her boot, he halted and steadied her arm. He was a man dedicated to his work, but he seemed in no hurry to return to it.

She could've been one of the farm wives escorting her husband home from the field. It would be easy to get used to. But Cormac was the one doing the escorting. And not home but back to her rented room.

A stronger spy wouldn't balk at the chance to seduce him in that room and delay his return to the worksite even further. A stronger woman wouldn't balk at the chance to explore this opportunity for lovemaking. It had been easy enough to lie on top of him in the mud. More than easy.

When they reached town, Cormac headed directly to her hotel and up to her room. Striding inside, he set her camera and valise on the floor by a chair. Her feet ached from their walk, but she refused to sit. Instead, she hovered by the door, racking her brain for a way to prevent his return to the worksite. He turned to leave.

She had to do something to keep him in this room. One thought rose above the chaos churning in her mind. He wouldn't leave if she was undressed. She shut the door and unfastened the top button of her dress.

Cormac froze. "Adella—"

"I need clean clothing." She leaned against the door and lowered her hand to the next button. Her hand trembled, questioning her impetuous decision. She pushed all thought aside save one. She must delay the railroad's construction. She opened the button.

Cormac sucked in his breath. "I'm not

letting you seduce me to get what you want." Despite his words, he didn't move to stop her.

Her fingers brushed the piece of paper hidden in her cleavage and she went as still as him. *Blast!* She'd forgotten about the telegram! She needed Cormac to stay in this room, but she couldn't let him see the telegram.

"How do you know what I want?" she whispered, stalling for time.

"I don't. But this is what I want." In two strides, he devoured the gap between them. Then his mouth claimed hers in a hot, heady possession.

Pressed against the door, all she could do was kiss him back. She did so with abandon. Her skin tingled, and her blood raced as if her body had woken from years of sleepwalking. She didn't want the feeling to stop. She wrapped her arms around Cormac's neck and pulled him closer.

He suddenly lifted his head. "I want more than one kiss," he murmured against her lips. "And I don't mean merely claiming everything that's under this dress." His hand slid up her ribcage to cup her breast.

The telegram! With a gasp, she covered her chest with both hands. The corner of the paper poked her palm. *Thank Dixie.* It was still there. But had he seen it? She drew back against the door.

Cormac retreated as well, lifting his hand to rake it through hair that was already disheveled. Had she done that? He reached for the doorknob and she jumped aside.

"Stay away from the worksite, Adella." He opened the door without his customary restraint. It banged against the wall. "And, for God's sake, stay out of trouble. Don't provoke a man beyond his patience."

Chapter 6

Glancing repeatedly at the ribbon of orange growing on the eastern horizon, Cormac slogged through the mud, making a beeline for the tent city. When he found the missing men, he'd blister them with a few choice words. Rather than delay the entire crew, he'd been forced to order the train to go to the worksite without him. His belly rumbled, already missing breakfast.

Rounding the corner of the mercantile, the field that held his and his men's homes came into view. In front of a broad swath of tents—crowded together so closely they resembled one gigantic sheet of canvas—rested a pair of wagons filled with men jostling each other for a better position. On the ground before them, someone in a skirt bent under a dark cloth draped over a camera. Parts of his body he had difficulty controlling of late instantly recognized the slim waist and curved bottom.

"Ready?" asked a muffled, but familiar voice from under the cloth.

Very ready.

The men assumed stilted poses. Adella pulled her head from the under the cloth. Her auburn hair, tousled and untamed, filled his thoughts with memories of her pressed against the length of him—both in the mud and in her hotel room. If only he didn't have work to do. If only he could forget she was a spy. A spy whose next move he couldn't predict any better than the first saboteur he still needed to catch.

A flash of light and puff of smoke yanked him from his musings.

Dragging his gaze from Adella, he focused on the scene before of him. Adella was a photographer after all. She had an artist's eye for picture taking. She'd positioned the men in front of the tents, the dawn light breaking over their heads, their wagons lined up to leave town. The scene hinted at a provocative story. He needed to learn the caption before he read it, along with everyone else, in the newspapers.

Damnation! If these men had failed to meet the morning train to the Katy worksite, but they were now assembled to leave town, then they might be defecting to the Joy Line. The rival railroad ran parallel to the Katy. The workmen could be there tomorrow. He needed to stop them.

His gaze locked with one of the men on the wagons. The man turned away, whispering to his friends and destroying his chance to catch them unaware and eavesdropping on any conversation. Soon all the men's heads were turned in his direction.

Adella glanced over her shoulder and went from relaxed to stiff as a rail.

Pinning his gaze on his men, his traitorous feet never-the-less brought him to a halt beside her, close enough to feel the warmth of her body and something else vibrating inside her. Was she remembering their kiss? He was.

"Nice morning for a photograph," he drawled. "Make a fine keepsake or gift to send the folks back home." People expected a man his size to also be thick in the head, to solve problems with his fists rather than his brains. On occasions like this, better to play dumb and say little of importance. He folded his arms and waited for his men or Adella to make the next move.

Her only response was a brisk rustling as she packed her camera.

"You can't stop us from leaving, McGrady," one of the men hollered.

"Stop you?" He raised his eyebrows as if the notion hadn't even entered his head. "Didn't realize you were going somewhere."

"The Joy Line's paying fifty cents more

than the Katy." The man drew a piece of paper from his pocket and waved it over his head. "This here telegram says so."

He should've known. Another point of contention fueled by money, or the lack of. But he didn't believe that Adella had become a spy for money. When he'd asked how much the Joy Line was paying her, she'd sidestepped the question and said: *I'm getting what I need.*

What did she need? Why was Stevens her enemy? Did it have something to do with her brother? He still didn't understand a thing about her. But he understood the men and agreed with them. They deserved fair compensation for their labor. They deserved whatever the competition was getting.

"Today, I'll use my own pay to cover the wage difference," he said. "You, and the men already at the worksite, will receive Joy Line wages." Adella's rustling stopped. He fought the urge to glance her way and gauge her reaction. "Whatever follows will be up to Stevens. If he won't pay, you can always leave tomorrow. And you'll have a pretty picture to impress all the ladies at your new workplace."

Nerves stretched taut, he waited for Adella's response. Not even a whisper of sound came from her direction. The men clustered closer together. The hum of their voices grated on his nerves, foreshadowing a counteroffer.

"My offer's only good for the next ten seconds. Don't make me split your raise amongst the men already heading to the worksite. Men who deal openly with me." He uncrossed his arms, so the men could see his fists. "Men who come to me with their concerns, rather than making me come after them."

The men sat down in the wagons, urging the horses to make haste. The first wagon paused when it pulled even with him. The man with the telegram thrust out his hand, offering the paper to Cormac.

Another delay diverted, thank the good God. He reached for the telegram but stopped midway. Diverted for how long? He understood workmen not spies. But he'd only gained that knowledge after five years working on the transcontinental. He didn't have years to learn to think like a spy. All he had was one spy discovered by accident. He had Adella. Could he learn by shadowing her? And in the process keep her out of trouble as well?

He let his hand drop to his side.

"Give the telegram to Stevens when you tell him what we discussed. Tell the McGrady Gang as well." He drew his watch from his waistcoat. "They'll let me know if you don't reach the worksite shortly."

The wagons rattled off toward the worksite. Feet stomped on the wooden walkway, heading in the opposite direction. He followed the footsteps.

Adella carried her camera wrapped in cloth and hanging from her shoulder in the rope sling he'd fashioned for it yesterday. The thought that he'd done something to make her life easier pleased him.

She also carried the bag he'd never seen her without. The tightness along her shoulders spoke louder than any outburst. Independent woman. Indomitable spy. Inexperienced seductress. None of her parts seemed big enough to define all of her. He wanted to know the woman beneath the façade.

Unfortunately, his first duty was to his work. He must learn what made a spy a spy. Soon he'd be forced to tighten the reins on Adella's activities. A sudden ache invaded his heart. He had no desire to dull her spirit. But the need to keep her and everyone else safe outweighed even his work obligations. He must learn as much as he could in the hope of corralling the railroad's unknown number of foes.

Hoping to broach that subject in a roundabout way, he said, "I'd bet money you're a first-rate photographer. Why not focus on those skills and stop provoking so much unrest?"

"Why not focus on being a foreman and stop following me?" Despite her brusque reply her pace slowed. "You're the oddest man I ever met. Sending those workers back with the telegram won't make your boss happy."

"Stevens' happiness isn't high on my list of priorities."

"Empowering your workmen might halt construction permanently. What kind of foreman wants that? Your gang said you were hired because you had a reputation for fast work."

"One can be fast and fair."

"One usually must decide between the two."

He'd had this conversation before—with himself—and his answer hadn't changed. "Then I choose fair."

She snorted. "You'll go broke giving your wages to others."

"At least I'll meet my maker with a clean conscience on that charge."

Adella's pace increased, until she was walking faster than when she'd first left the tent city. He cursed himself under his breath. If he'd learned anything from his brief time with Adella, it was that pushing too hard made her as approachable as a prickly hedgehog.

Struggling for a way to soften his unintentional reproach, he ended up following her in silence. She wore a pretty but simple gingham dress. Its plainness didn't stop him from becoming mesmerized by the sway of her hips. After a while the footpath stopped branching and led to only one destination—the livery. She'd planned to ride somewhere. That was why she was dressed so practically today. She did everything for a reason.

"Where we heading?" he asked.

"*We* are headed nowhere. I've decided to take your advice and be a photographer today. Your railroad is safe from me. Return to it."

"I don't like you wandering around alone. Too many rough men who could take advantage."

"I've been wandering through worse places since I was fifteen. Besides, thanks to you, all the rough men are now at the worksite."

He shrugged. "One can never be too sure."

"True." She glanced over her shoulder. "You're still in town."

"I shall escort you wherever you like." He wouldn't mind escorting her back to her hotel room and continuing where they'd left off. But that would be another game for Adella. When he took her to bed, he wanted her to be there for only one reason. Him.

"You don't even know where I'm going."

"You could tell me."

She turned her gaze forward, dismissing him. "I could, but I don't have to. More importantly I don't want to. I can look after myself. Why are you still here?" Although her voice remained neutral, her body tensed with sudden interest. "Are there additional delays beyond a few missing workers? Has construction shut down?"

"That's another good thing about the McGrady Gang. They can push forward without me for a few hours. I'm free to assist you."

"I don't like being followed. You make me feel—" She clamped her mouth shut and bowed her head as if she regretted her words.

What, Adella? What do I make you feel?

Spinning to face him head-on, she deposited her camera and bag on the walkway, creating a wall between them. "If I don't move, you can't follow me." She folded her arms and her lips flattened into a determined line. "I can stand here all day."

"I have a better idea." He scooped up her belongings. Ignoring her startled gasp, he stepped down into the mud and walked around her. Then he regained the footpath and continued on toward the livery. "Why don't you follow me for a change?"

After Cormac procured horses at the livery, Adella followed him east. When their mounts broke free of the mud and found firmer ground outside of town, she urged her mount into a trot.

Despite Cormac's comment about her following him, he rode only slightly ahead while carrying her camera and valise. He maneuvered his horse close to hers, matching her pace, leading her while still staying next to her—as he'd done yesterday when they'd walked together. She rode astride, her skirt hiked up to her knees, showing an unladylike amount of stocking-clad leg.

His gaze sought her often, but each time he looked away just as quickly...until he caught her contemplating him in return. "'Tis good you finally decided to photograph the farm widows for real."

She'd seen too many women suffer during the war and had never held the power to help them. Her guilt for failing the widows had hounded her all night. As had her fascination for Cormac. She couldn't do anything about the later except try to camouflage her ardor with shrewish comments.

"It's good that you're familiar with horses," she replied, "and won't slow me down." Her lack of sleep should've helped sharpen her tone. Instead, her voice sounded unaccountably pleased.

He lifted one shoulder in a shrug. "I come from a family of tenant farmers."

His humble description breached her defenses. She laughed. "You know more than the backside of a plow horse."

A smile curved his mouth, making her feel like a family of grasshoppers danced around her belly. "Back home—when it rained and the landlord's children stayed snug in their home—me and my sister borrowed their ponies and raced across the moors." A frown twisted his brow and the joy vanished from his lips. "There were many rainy days in Galway."

Cormac must miss his family. Even though he'd visited Ireland only a few months ago, it'd be a long time before he could make a return trip. He might never see his family again. A shared sadness tightened her chest.

She tried to infuse her voice with lightness. "You and your sister were a pair of rapscallion children." She knew the kind well, but only in memories. Luckily those particular memories were good ones.

"Molly was three years older than me and wise beyond measure." Cormac's tone was subdued. "I did everything she told me to do, until she was twelve."

Unease, chill as a north wind, froze her. "And after that?"

"We had no more time for games." Cormac nudged his horse into a canter.

Adella did the same. His pace left no room for conversations but wasn't so fast it put either her or her camera in danger. Had his sister taught him that?

Land covered in stubble turned brown and brittle from the winter, stretched around them as far as the eye could see. Liberating after the muddy town, the earth here held the promise of new life, of change. But the wind, briskly pushing the ever-present clouds overhead, warned how unsettling change might be.

On the horizon a dot grew larger, turning into several dots: a farmhouse, barn and chicken coop. From the house came a tall figure with white-blonde hair contrasting starkly with the brown earth and the gray sky.

Cormac slowed his horse to a walk. "Your photographs might help Helga."

Adella's hands tightened on her reins. She hadn't come to New Chicago for photographs. Cormac knew that now, but he continued trying to save her and everyone else around him. "Your sister taught you well," she said. "To ride and to do what's right."

"That didn't stop Molly from dying. I

didn't do anything right then."

His sister had died? Cormac's words at the worksite came back to her. *I won't let anyone else die because of me.* Good God, he believed he'd caused his sister's death? How?

Before she could ask, Helga called, "Isn't this a merry surprise, the two of you visiting me together?"

They rode the remaining distance in silence. Cormac greeted Helga politely, then dismounted and unstrapped Adella's camera from his saddle.

With his back turned, Helga cast Adella a questioning glance.

She busied herself climbing down from her horse.

"Never expected to be in so many pictures," Helga said. "A body could get famous this way."

"Or infamous," Cormac replied. "I'm sure Miss Willows has the ability to make either happen." With her camera under one arm, he turned to face Adella. "Well, have you made up your mind?"

She blinked in confusion. All she could think about was his sister. "Made up my mind about what?"

He gestured in a broad arc that encompassed the farm buildings. "About what backdrop you'll choose for your next picture."

She turned to Helga. "I'd like to keep things as homey as possible. What were you planning to do before we arrived?"

"Got a basket of washing that needs hanging."

Adella nodded. "A full laundry line with the house behind will do nicely."

Helga took the camera from Cormac. "We ladies have things in order. I could use some more wood chopped, though." She thrust her chin in the direction of the house.

Cormac's brows raised at the stack of wood piled high against one wall. Enough wood to last a year. He hesitated as if he wanted to say something. Then he strode toward his assignment. Had his sister taught him this as well? Not to argue when a woman requested help? What had happened to her?

That one question filled her mind, leaving room for nothing else. She took a step to follow Cormac.

Helga dumped the camera in her arms, halting her. "Set up wherever you like while I fetch my basket."

With the whack of Cormac's axe creating an unbroken rhythm in the background, Adella assembled her camera and joined Helga in hanging laundry as white as the widow's hair. When Adella reached for the last sheet in the basket, Helga seized her wrist.

Another unexplainable jolt of apprehension, similar to when Helga took hold of her in the missionary tent, rocked Adella. Why did Helga affect her thus? Was it the woman's swiftness, her determination, her blunt manner? All three made a formidable personality. Still, Adella reminded herself, Helga was not a threat. She was not her enemy.

"Leave that for later." Helga released Adella and set the basket on her hip.

Exhaling slowly to steady her nerves and hands, Adella returned to her camera. She repositioned the tripod several times, before she was satisfied with what she saw through the viewfinder—a once thriving home now attended by a sole occupant. Without husband or children or even livestock to stand beside Helga, the shot took on a melancholy tone.

"Ready?" she called to Helga. "Remember not to move."

A sudden surge of uncertainty held her immobile as well. Had everything she'd done since Declan's death been meaningless? Was she living her life for the wrong reasons? Before her stood a flesh and blood person who needed her help, not a ghost who couldn't be saved or even avenged. Not properly at least. The dead remained dead. There was no changing that.

She took the picture in a hurry and bundled up the camera even faster.

With her basket still in hand, Helga moved to stand beside her. "Now that that's done, I want you to see something." Glancing over her shoulder at Cormac, who continued chopping wood with an untiring stroke, Helga positioned her broad bulk between them. Then she lifted the sheet from the basket. Three sticks of dynamite lay underneath.

Shock paralyzed Adella. "What're you doing with that?"

"If there's no track, my farm's worth nothing to nobody but me."

An image of a crater torn in the earth—blackened rails and bloodied men lying battered and broken around it—flashed before her eyes. The McGrady Gang would lie among them and Cormac too. Ears ringing and body swaying from a blast that had yet to happen, she latched onto Helga's arm. "Please tell me you don't mean to blow up the worksite."

"Thought about it, but I can't chance hurting my supplier. Might need more of these." Helga caressed the dynamite in her basket with a lover's hand.

Adella felt her jaw drop. "You're working with someone from the Katy? Why would he sabotage his own workplace?"

"He didn't say. Only said he didn't want another incident like yours at the station."

Astonishment robbed her ability to speak, but her thoughts raced like the clouds across the sky. Did Helga know the man who'd dumped the load that nearly killed Adella? Her blood felt like ice and so did the future. She wrapped her arms around herself.

Cormac's axe was suddenly silent.

Helga returned the sheet to the basket and said in rushed whisper, "Just wanted you to know, so you'd be ready with your camera." Then she stepped aside so Adella saw Cormac again, and him her.

He stood, axe in hand, frowning at them. His gaze swept over her, almost as if searching for an injury. When he didn't find anything amiss, his stance lost some of its rigidity. He glanced at Helga, his brow lowering even further. Then he slammed his axe into a log and strode toward them. Behind him, the stack of wood had grown with freshly cut wood piled atop.

Its size had been sufficient when Cormac started. Helga was as strong as a man. She didn't require help splitting wood. The no-nonsense Irishman striding toward them knew this, but he'd still accepted the task. Not just out of habit from a sister's training or out of politeness to a stranger like Helga. He'd done it to give Adella room and trust.

And she'd used that trust to discover something that might not only harm his railroad but him. She held information that might kill him. The clammy hand of fear brushed her skin.

Thunder rumbled on the horizon. "Rain's finally coming," Helga said.

Adella spun to face her. "When will—?"

"Soon. Like we discussed yesterday, it's best to work when the season's ripe."

Cormac had crossed half the distance separating them. Little time remained.

"Tell me who you're working with," Adella whispered.

"He told me not to say."

"Helga, please be careful. You don't want to hurt anyone, or get hurt. This man you're dealing with, he might be a spy for the Joy Line."

"He's no threat to me. I'm stronger than him, than all of them." Helga's lips pressed into a hard line.

Cormac was within hearing distance. His gaze shifted momentarily from them to the sky. "We'd better head for town," he said.

Adella nodded, grateful for his steady hands as he carried her camera to their horses and secured it on his saddle. Her own hands shook as she mounted her horse. She wanted to turn her horse east and run away from everyone she'd met since coming to New Chicago. Instead, she waved farewell to Helga and kept her horse no faster than a trot as she and Cormac rode west in the direction of town.

When she glanced back and saw Helga disappear inside her house, she gave in to her screaming nerves and urged her horse into a gallop. Seemingly in response, the sky opened up and rain pelted her skin like fierce pinpricks, pushing her to even greater speed.

Cormac was suddenly beside her. Grabbing her reins, he slowed her horse. "We won't make it to town. Not before the worst of the storm hits. We must take shelter and wait it out." He jerked his head to the left. "There's an abandoned farm over that knoll."

They clattered across a creek rising with the rain and clambered up the slope. The rain now fell thick, obscuring her view. Their horses skidded down the other side, sliding in earth slick with puddles. Lightning lit the horizon, granting her a glimpse of a ramshackle house with its door agape and banging in the wind. Seconds later, thunder boomed. Then the heavens unleashed a bruising deluge.

"The barn's that way," Cormac yelled. "Let's get the horses inside."

Before the last word had left his lips, she was turning her horse blindly in the direction he'd indicated. The barn held little more than a pile of hay with two stalls opposite. After they'd seen to their mounts, it only took a few strides to stand by the door. The rain had halted, but the clouds circled, preparing for another assault.

The sodden gingham of her dress clung to her, heavy and revealing. She wanted to run, to hide, to disappear. The storm and now the cramped barn, made even smaller by Cormac's size, thwarted her.

She dared not look at him for fear of seeing what his clothing revealed. Wet linen and tweed plastered to a solid, muscular body would torment her. She yearned to run her hands over him, stroke every line and swell. But she also wanted to delve deeper and discover what secrets he harbored as well.

She released a pained sigh. Other than their one all-too-brief kiss inside her hotel room, he'd met her advances with rejection. Or worse concern and questions. And she had told him too much already.

He moved closer. He didn't touch her, but the heat of his body pulled at her just the same. She propped one shoulder against the doorjamb, using it as an anchor.

"We should make a run for the house," he said.

"That would be trespassing."

"Its owner is long gone. When a railroad

reaches a town, some folks pack up and hop on the train. Some say they're heading east to a better life."

Adella could've told them there wasn't anything better in the East. Ghosts and regrets followed wherever you went. Same with new troubles. They sprouted like thistles in a vegetable patch. The door across the yard started banging again, driven by the wind, which was rising to its previous howl.

"We'd be better off inside the house," Cormac said. "You're soaked through. You're shivering."

She remembered another time when she'd been drenched and watching a house in the unforgiving rain. "I won't go inside. It's still someone's home. They might come back."

"That's unlikely."

"*I* came back."

A weighty silence hung between them, amplified by the storm outside the barn, before Cormac asked, "After the war?"

She shook her head, making her sodden hair tumble loose from its pins. "After the war, when the carpetbaggers overran the south, my home was long gone." Thick locks slid down her cheeks. She left them there, using them as a shield as she peered sideways at Cormac. "This was *during* the war when the Yankee troops first started paying house calls."

He reached out to touch her, but stopped. His hand fell in a fist by his side. "The soldiers— Did they— find you inside?"

"No. I hid in the trees like a coward and watched a noble band of Union Blue tear up the walls of my two-room house to fill the fireplaces in the plantation mansion. Squatters and thieves. To them, my home was just kindling. Although the big house didn't fare any better two years later during Sherman's march."

He put his hand on her shoulder then, pulling her out of the past into the present. "What did Helga say to you?"

Desperation to feel something new, rather than wallowing in the past, overwhelmed her. She spun to face him. "I'm tired of talking. Show me what would've happened in the hotel if we hadn't stopped."

"You don't really want that, lass."

"I do." The intensity of her response made him draw back in surprise. It surprised her too. She was surprised she'd resisted his appeal this long.

"What if you get pregnant?" he demanded. "I refuse to bring a child into this world that won't be properly cared for by a mother and father united as one, not just on paper but in their hearts. Can you do that, lass?"

The enormity of his proposal made her head spin. She couldn't have heard him correctly. Only his first question seemed answerable. A long ago snippet of conversation gathered while eavesdropping rose to her rescue. Maybe all her listening and lurking hadn't been for naught.

"The men in the army talked about pulling out at the last, spilling their seed on the ground...if they had a care for a woman and she asked."

Swearing again in Gaelic, Cormac pressed his fingers to the bridge of his nose. "You shouldn't have heard that."

"But I did and I'm asking."

"You ask too much. It'd be too hard a thing to remember when I've got the prettiest lass I've ever seen in my arms."

She moved closer to him. She craved his warmth, his strength, his touch. She didn't want to run from this. "I'll remember for both of us."

"You could do this with any man. Why me?"

She wanted to delay his return to the worksite. No. That was a lie, with them trapped in the barn and his men probably all hunkered down themselves to wait out the storm. Sometimes it was easier to tell oneself lies. And sometimes it was easier to say aloud just a little bit of the truth.

She placed her palm on his chest. "I

want you."

The muscles in his jaw jerked taut as leather. He stomped away. Flopping down on his back on the pile of hay, he threw one arm over his eyes.

She followed and sat beside him. She made sure not to touch him. She didn't want him retreating again. "Is this your way of telling me no?"

"You ask too much. I want more than a quick toss, lass. I want that child I spoke of. I want a family again."

The yearning in his voice made her stomach churn with apprehension. She hugged her knees to her chest and propped her chin on them. "When you went home to Ireland..." She wanted to ask if a sweetheart had been waiting for him. Her courage failed her. "You went back to start a family?"

"No. I returned to help the family I'd left. I went back for my sister, Meghan." He thrust his fingers deep into his hair and left them there. He stared at the roof without blinking. "I told you my sister, Molly, died. She wasn't the only one."

His words chilled her.

Shaking as if cold as well, he continued in a strangled voice, "During the two years following Molly's death, my sisters—Muriel and Maeve and Maureen—died. Meghan only survived by a hairsbreadth."

Tears blurred her eyes. "And your parents?"

"I was told my mother died when I was four. A year later, my father didn't return from the tavern. That was one of my first memories. Not his failure to come home, but my sisters all saying it'd be easier without him. But the McGrady sisters never had things easy." His skin had turned as white as bleached bone.

When he'd said people died because of him, he'd meant his sisters. She didn't believe it. "How did they die?"

"*An Gorta Mór.* The Great Hunger. It took everyone I loved except Meghan."

Despite her sorrow for his loss, she breathed a sigh of relief. He wasn't responsible for anyone's death. He wasn't like Levi Parsons. "You can't blame yourself for surviving a country-wide famine that happened...how long ago?"

"Molly died in '48, a few years after the potato blight hit. She was only twelve. I should've—"

"Wait! That's when you said you stopped riding the landlord's ponies. You said Molly was twelve. Just three years older than you. My God. You were only a boy when she died!"

"It would've been better if I'd never been born. Then they'd have had more to eat. They'd have lived."

"You don't know that!" Her voice was sharper than she'd intended.

"Aye, I do. After Molly passed, my eldest sister, Muriel, wouldn't speak for a fortnight. When she finally did, it was to assemble us around Molly's grave and pledge that no one younger than she would die. She was looking at me when she said it. Each of my sisters made the same vow when she became the eldest. They died because of me."

"They made their own decisions."

"I didn't fully understand what they were doing at first. Then, later, I didn't even have the brains to steal a loaf of bread without getting caught." His voice was flat as if he spoke about someone other than himself. "The parish constable, a kindly sort who could've jailed or transported me, blistered my palms with a leather strap. Couldn't pick up, let alone pinch, anything for weeks. Then, by dumb luck, I found work. Earned enough to buy the bread I was so useless at stealing. I've worked every day since."

He drew in a deep breath as if steeling himself to continue. "But I started too late. By then only Meghan was alive." He finally looked at her. The silver of his eyes had turned a shade as dark and unforgiving as the clouds holding them prisoner in the barn.

"My sisters' resolve terrified me. So did my failure to do anything to save them. I feel the same way about you."

Chapter 7

God rot his sorry soul. Why had he burdened Adella with all his weaknesses? He'd never bared his soul so completely to anyone. If asked about his trip to Galway, he'd just said he had five sisters and was going home to help the one who still needed him.

Only when he got back, Meghan—true to the McGrady sisters' pluck—hadn't needed him. His five-year absence, finally earning a decent wage on the transcontinental railroad and sending every penny home, had given Meghan space. Space to stop clinging to the past and hovering over a baby brother who now, at age thirty-one, towered over her.

Meghan had found a husband who Cormac grudgingly respected, had given birth to a boy of her own, and had a second child on the way. She'd built a new family. After returning his money, she urged him to do the same.

Uncurling from her sitting position, Adella stretched out on her back beside him. His arms ached to hold her. All of her. Every lithe curve. Even her determined, and often sharp, knees and elbows.

She took a turn at staring at the roof.

"What are you thinking?" he asked, craving the sound of her voice

"That you had a gang long before you came to America and started building railroads."

He didn't know what he'd expected, but not that. He laughed, not a happy laugh but still a laugh. It eased some of the tightness gripping his chest.

She rolled on her side and met his gaze. Even sopping-wet she was damned pretty. She stole his breath and made it hard to think of anything but her, which was a blessing right now.

"I'm also thinking that you learned to take care of those in need from the very best. Yesterday, when you told Stevens to pay the farm widows or leave them alone, you were remembering your sisters."

"I suppose so."

She shimmied closer, her breasts grazing his side. His arm instinctively dropped down around her shoulders. He kept his grip loose, waiting for her retreat, dreading it.

Instead, she slid on top of him. Desire shot through him hard and fast, making his whole frame stiffen.

"You make a nice island," she murmured.

He forced his body to relax. Not all of him would listen.

"An Irish island in a sea of American mud?" He lowered his voice to match hers. "Will you stay with me?" He threaded his fingers in her hair and searched her eyes. "Will you think of the future rather than the past? Whatever happened, whatever turned you into a spy, it's not too late to do something different." His hold on her involuntarily tightened. "Build a life with me."

Shadows danced across her golden eyes. Ghosts tormented her as well. "Like a milkmaid stumbling across a giant sleeping in her barn, I should really run for my life."

But Adella wasn't running. She remained in his arms. "You aren't one of those easily intimidated maidens."

"In this barn, if I asked again, would my giant become my lover?"

He flinched, nearly toppling her off him. He stared at her, too stunned to even curse. Then a slow certainty stole over him, gentling his grip on her. If he couldn't have Adella, then he didn't want a family. And he couldn't change Adella. He could only accept her, love her, and cherish every moment he was blessed with her in his arms. He uncurled his fingers, releasing her hair, smoothing the auburn locks, arranging the thick mass over her shoulders and down her spine.

She cocked her head, frowning down at him warily, awaiting his answer.

"Have you lain with a man before?"

She shook her head. "Does it matter?"

"Yes." He pulled a wayward curl of her hair, a teasing gesture he'd seen Meghan's husband do in Galway. He didn't want to hurt Adella in any way. He must go slowly with her.

"You still won't grant my request." She squeezed shut her eyes and pulled away from him. "I think it's time to rise and face the reality."

"I think not." In one swift movement, he lifted his head and pressed his lips to hers. So much for proceeding slowly.

He swallowed her surprised gasp, then her moan of pleasure. With the gap between them finally removed, he succumbed to the fierce need he'd been holding back. She returned his kiss with equal passion. Scorching him, enticing him, amazing him. Whenever Adella decided to do something, she did it boldly.

Lungs burning, he slid his lips along her cheek. He needed to catch his breath, but he couldn't stop touching her. He rubbed the curve of his cheekbone against her soft cheek, delighting in her throaty purr. With his hands cradling her head, he explored the ridge of her jaw, the pulse point at the end, the hollow below her ear. She arched her back, granting him better access.

He slowed his movements, wanting to remember everything about this moment. He inhaled deeply, drawing in the scent of her warm skin mixed with the flower of her perfume. The rain droplets, beading on her skin, were sweet on his tongue.

She trembled against him and arched her back even more. His lips found the swell of her breasts. Unrestrained breasts. She wasn't wearing a corset. Sliding his hands down, he cupped her breasts, one in each palm. They were the perfect size and shape for his thumb to caress her nipples through her wet dress. They pebbled immediately. He unbuttoned her bodice and slipped his hands under her chemise. Flesh against flesh. So soft, so beautiful. His mouth swiftly followed his hands.

His blood pounded in his ears and raced to his groin. She rubbed her pelvis against his, and his hands immediately shot down to cover her bottom and press her firm against his erection. The growl in the back of his throat startled him.

"You know how to test a man's restraint

in the best way possible, lass. Rock your hips like this." He guided her in the rhythm he craved. She was a damned quick study. The pleasure she wrenched from him left him struggling to hold onto what little remained of his control. And all with her still clothed. What would it feel like with her naked against him?

"You'll remember to pull out? At the end?" Her voice was breathless and husky, driving him to the precipice.

He didn't want to think about the end. Doing so might send him over the edge right now. He rolled her onto her back and lifted the hem of her skirt. "No. I doubt if I'd remember," he whispered close to her ear. "So I'm going to make love to you another way."

He glided his fingers up the intoxicatingly soft skin of her inner thigh, pausing to trace circles, advancing, retreating but always moving higher. Delicious shivers rippled through her body as she opened to him.

He didn't stop until she cried out his name and arched tight as a bowstring against his hand. Wrapping her in his arms, he concentrated on counting to one hundred. He wasn't ruining this one perfect moment with her. It might be all he ever had.

"I had no idea that was possible," she

murmured.

With Adella in his arms, the world outside was hushed, silent. He lifted his head. No, it wasn't just the peace of being with her. The wind and rain no longer rattled the rafters. The storm had stopped. He was being selfish, continuing to hold Adella while she wore a damp dress in a drafty barn.

He pulled down her skirt and buttoned her bodice. "We should head for town and find you some dry clothes."

"We're not...continuing?"

"You need time to think, to decide."

"I do?" She ducked her head, avoiding his gaze. "Or you do?"

He laced his fingers with hers and rose, pulling her to her feet beside him. "I know what I want."

She still wouldn't meet his gaze. Instead, she stared at their linked hands and said, "You once said I should come find you if I needed help."

"You still should. No matter what you decide about..." he squeezed her fingers, "...this." He immediately loosened his grip, so she could pull free if she wanted. "I'll move my tent away from the others so that if you need assistance, you can find me quickly."

"What if I just need...you?" She lifted her head.

The unblinking intensity in her amber eyes made his chest swell with hope. Maybe, just maybe, he could steal happiness one moment at a time with her. "Then come to me tonight. I'll be waiting."

Riding beside Adella, Cormac pointed his mount in the direction of New Chicago. He let the horse choose its own pace across a ravine fetlock-deep in water. It would take hours, maybe days, for this much rain to soak into the earth.

Adella's unbound hair spilled down her back, swaying in the wake of the wind that drove the darkest clouds over the horizon. Her beauty stole his breath like his first glimpse of Ireland after five long years away. He'd been hopeful then as well. And it had all come to naught.

A baritone boom shook the earth.

"Another thunderstorm?" She craned her neck, inspecting the sky.

He did the same. The eastern horizon flickered bright orange. Then black smoke billowed, obscuring the light.

He turned his horse sharply, urging it toward this new cloud. Adella's horse splashed close behind him. The hoof beats matched his own mount's stride for stride when he cleared the water and rode as fast as he dared up the soft, slippery slope.

On the other side, in a broad valley, lay the smoke's source—the fractured boiler of a locomotive burrowed in the earth to its running boards. Behind it, a boxcar lay on its side. Then came a car reduced to kindling by a final freight car. Iron rails, identical to those that had nearly crushed Adella, lay scattered like match sticks.

In the middle of the destruction, a section of the track had collapsed underwater. Guilt tore through his gut. His shoddy work, his failure to defy Stevens' continued demands to increase the pace of construction, had done this. Where was the train's crew? Were they dead?

He raced down the hill without a thought for his own well-being. Leaping from his horse, he climbed onto the engine. The cab was empty. From his vantage point, he spun in a circle searching, gasping for air like a drowning man. His gaze halted on Adella kneeling next to a figure stretched on the ground behind the wreck. He stopped breathing all together.

She lifted her head, her gaze meeting his. She smiled and beckoned for him to join her.

"Thank Dixie you're alive," she said to the man on the ground as Cormac skidded to a halt beside them.

"How's my train?" the man asked on groan.

"The storm roughed her up a bit. But it's—" she paused until Cormac met her gaze again, "—nothing that can't be fixed."

Was his guilt written that plainly on his face?

"Nature didn't do this all on her own," the conductor said, shaking his head. "Men helped. After we came off the rails, I saw three of them swoop into the first boxcar, quick as buzzards."

"What was inside?" she asked.

"The payroll," Cormac replied.

Without that money half the workmen would jump ship for the Joy Line. Hell, they'd all leave, except for maybe the McGrady Gang. And he couldn't let his gang stay if they weren't getting paid. Things couldn't get any worse.

"Thank Jesus," the conductor said, "we didn't pick up the passenger car at the last town."

Cormac spat out a curse. Things could always get worse. And so far he hadn't done a damned thing to stop them. "When I find these saboteurs, I'll make sure they're locked up with the key buried. They can stay there till they—"

Adella's face had turned ashen. Regret bombarded his heart. Instinctively, he reached for her. She retreated and stared without blinking at the wreckage.

Shoving his outstretched hands in his

pockets, he pivoted to face the man on the ground. "Can you tell us what the robbers looked like?"

The conductor shook his head. "Too much smoke and they'd covered their faces with bandanas."

Cormac's thoughts spun, grappling for answers. "Did they say anything?"

"Yeah, but it was mighty strange. I only understood the one phrase."

"Which was?"

"As they rode off, one of them yelled: *To tyrants we'll not yield.*"

Adella sucked in a breath.

Why? The words didn't mean a thing to him. He studied the conductor. "You sure? You were thrown pretty far from the train and—"

"Course I'm bloody sure!" The conductor cast Adella an apologetic glance. "Sorry, miss. I still get riled when I hear the old battle cries. Heard 'em too many times when a wave of Rebel Gray charged and started riddling my troop with bullets."

Cormac frowned. The conductor's comments felt contradictory. "So why call their words strange?"

"Because everything they said before that was gibberish. They were talking in Irish."

Adella's valise felt heavy as a mortar shell, as she crept along the footpath. Could she use the valise's contents to pacify rather than provoke? To heal rather than harm? The night was as black as the conservatively-cut mourning dress she'd chosen to wear. Bulky clouds still hung overhead, preventing the moon and stars from showing her the way. The only light came from the workmen's tents ahead.

Had Cormac placed his tent away from the others, so she could find him? She doubted it. Not after the train wreck and his words there. It didn't matter. She wasn't searching for him.

The tents' peaked backs glowed from within. The flickering lantern light pulled her forward like a moth to the flame. *Fergal won't hurt me.* He wasn't one of the train robbers. He couldn't be. With his injured leg he couldn't ride with a mob, or clamor onto an overturned boxcar or help carry off a hefty payroll.

But the song... The Confederate *Battle Cry of Freedom* kept playing in her head.

They have laid down their lives
On the bloody battle field,
Shout, shout the battle cry of Freedom!
Their motto is resistance—
To tyrants we'll not yield!

The last line ground her hopes to dust.

One of the outlaws was an Irish speaking Rebel soldier.

There'd been plenty of Irishmen in the war—on the Union side. In New York, the Yankees had recruited them straight off the immigrant ships. If one of these men had found his way to the other side, would he still shout a Rebel battle cry five years later? Would he cling to the song as tenaciously as a soldier born to the land? A son of the south like Fergal who could speak Irish as fluently as English?

Or maybe Fergal had taught the song to the workmen to rile them up. Could Fergal be an instigator, like her? What if she herself had said or done something that provoked those men into committing such a dangerous act? She wasn't concerned with the loss of the payroll, but the loss of the train crew—

Fortunately, after they'd found the conductor, they'd unearthed the brakeman and fireman as well. Battered and shaken, but alive. This time.

She had to find Fergal and reason with him. One of these tents was his, and one was Cormac's. Cormac, who for a day, had overlooked her being a spy. He wouldn't any longer. His words at the train wreck, his outrage and determination, stung her again. She and Cormac were enemies in a new type of war, an underhanded one. Maybe it was better to shout a war cry and charge directly at your opponent. At least then everyone knew where they stood.

Too many lies. Too many secrets. Too many regrets.

She couldn't live this life anymore. Not if it turned her into a murderer, or an accomplice to one. If Fergal was involved, she needed to stop him from harming anyone else, including himself. She had to find him.

Halting at the end of the last street that opened onto the tent city, she began her vigil. The mercantile loomed beside her. If the clouds decided to part, it would create a nice shadow in which to hide. The seconds ticked away in accompaniment to her pounding heart, until she lost track of the time.

"Are you looking for me?" The voice came from behind her.

She whipped around. "Fergal! You startled me."

He grabbed her arm and pulled her toward the tents. The ease with which he moved doubled her surprise, making her stiffen. He wasn't limping. His hold on her arm tightened, as if he sensed the change in her as well. He pulled her inside one of the tents and stood between her and the flap.

"Your leg," she whispered. "It was a lie?" Shock turned to horror as her life, and her resolve to ruin Parsons and avenge Declan, derailed as abruptly as this afternoon's train. "What else about Camp Douglas was a lie?"

"Everything that happened there was true. I was shot. The doctor didn't remove the bullet. Declan died in a cell. I almost did as well. But the war ended too early to grant me that release. When the gates were thrown open, I hobbled out of Camp Douglas with a limp. My body healed as best as it could, but a couple of months ago I injured my leg again and this time gangrene threatened. Once more, I was dying but this time I was alone."

"Alone?" Her usually cooperative brain refused to function. "Where was Cormac?"

"We'd completed the transcontinental and gone our separate ways. He headed to Ireland, and I decided to drink myself into oblivion." Fergal laughed a harsh self-deprecating sound. "Coward that I am, when faced again with my own death—by a festering broken leg—I suddenly wanted to live. Fortunately, this time around I had power. I had enough money to persuade a doctor to dig out the old bullet and set the bone...rather than look the other way and leave me to die. I also had time to heal, and to think. That's when I decided to come work for the Katy."

"But why act injured when you aren't?"

"So I wouldn't be suspected of my other activities."

Her mind blanked again, rejecting his words. "Fergal, no. You can't want to—"

"I do. And you do too. Otherwise why are you here? We're here because we both came to the same conclusion about the war, Dec's death and his killer. We must do everything we can to make that Yankee pay for his sins."

"I want him to pay as well. Creating delays, making him lose money. I hoped my ill-deeds would end there. But they don't. Those men on the train could've been killed."

"Causalities are inevitable in war."

Pain sliced her, sharp as the day she'd received the news of her brother's death. "Causalities like Declan?"

He jerked as if she'd wounded him as well. "You said you didn't want to talk about him."

"I was wrong. By never speaking of Declan I forgot who he was. I've spent the last hour rereading his letters." She extracted the bundle from its special compartment and tossed the valise aside.

"This is all that's important." She touched the letters reverently. "I'd forgotten how Declan craved peace. All throughout the war he wrote about it, about his hopes for coming home, about rebuilding rather than destroying."

She pressed the letters into Fergal's hands. "He wrote about you reciting the *Battle Cry of Freedom*. He wrote about his worry for you. He wrote how the war had changed you and to him that was the greatest loss of all. Then...he asked me to look after you, and he stopped writing. But I was selfish, wallowing in my grief and revenge. I never even looked for you."

Fergal frowned at the letters. "He asked me to take care of you as well. But you've never needed that. You're stronger than us all."

She shook her head. Her strength was an act, like Fergal's limp. A ruse to keep others at a distance.

"He's arriving in New Chicago on the next train." Fergal's words yanked her from her thoughts.

She blinked. "Who?"

"The rich Yankee responsible for Dec's death. He won't be leaving town."

No! She wouldn't be responsible for more death. Not even Parsons'. "I can't let you do this."

"You can't stop me."

"What if others get in the way and you kill them too?"

He frowned at her. "Stay away from the

train station, Adella."

"I don't mean me. I mean people like the crew on that train."

"You're all grown up, Adella, but you remain that little girl from Georgia who went out of her way not to step on flowers. Sometimes you have to crush a few stalks to get where you're going." Fergal held Declan's letters out to her. "You need these more than me."

She wrapped her hands around his, pressing his fingers tight against the letters. "You're wrong. You need Declan's words just as much as I do. Read them. Remember him."

Behind her, the tent flap jerked open with a snap. Cormac's giant frame shoved through the narrow gap. The scowl on his face was ten times fiercer than any she'd ever seen.

Chapter 8

Cormac halted inside the tent, staring at Adella pressing a packet of letters into Fergal's hands. His fury lessened just a fraction, allowing him to think. She wasn't hurt. He wouldn't have to attend anyone's funeral—namely Fergal's. Adella looked ready for one, though. She wore the black dress of a mourner and the ashen face of the deceased.

"What're you doing here?" Fergal growled. The last time he'd heard that particular tone was when Fergal had been drunk and cursing Adella's father.

"The men reported raised voices. They mentioned a woman's voice." The McGrady Gang said they'd heard Adella pleading with Fergal. The thought still made his temper spike. Praised be the Saints that his gang had come to him.

"You've interrupted a..." Fergal's gaze slid from him to Adella and back again,

"...lover's quarrel."

She jerked away from Fergal, her face flushing scarlet in the lantern light. "I have no idea who you are anymore. You certainly aren't the friend from my youth." She squeezed past Cormac and out of the tent.

Turning to follow her, his gaze snagged on her bag lying forgotten on the floor. He paused to grab the handle. The already opened bag released a stream of photographs and papers. Cursing, he knelt and stuffed them back inside.

"Adella, wait! You forgot—" He leapt outside...and lost her. Fingers numb, he dropped the bag and plunged into the night. Eyes straining for a glimpse of her, he followed the footpath—and hopefully Adella—into the center of New Chicago.

Worry seized his heart with the strength of a vulture's talons. How would he find her in this rabbit warren of side streets and back alleys? Should he head straight for her hotel? Muffled piano music sounded up ahead. Then the usual male guffaws that were never far from Eden's establishment. Should he go in and ask if she'd seen Adella?

A curse came from the alley alongside Eden's, followed by a scream, the crack of a slap, and then a man's voice.

"Bite me again and I'll hit you twice as hard. If yer found outside a brothel, especially at night, yer looking for a customer."

Cormac tore down the alley. A lantern sat on the ground beside three men crouched over a struggling woman. One pressed his hand over her mouth. Another pinned her arms above her head. The last man shoved up her skirt. The white of Adella's petticoats flashed stark against the black of that dress.

He slammed into the men with a roar. Kicked the first man in the ribs. Punched the second in the jaw. Kneed the third in the face. The final strike was the most satisfying as he thought he heard bone break and it set Adella free. She scrambled to her feet. A red handprint marred her pale cheek. A cheek already starting to bruise.

Swift as a spark touching gunpowder, his rage exploded. He spun to face her abusers, hands clenched ready to inflict more damage.

The men stood together. Cowards always found bravery in numbers.

"You should have brought more than muscle to this fight," one of them said. "You should've brought a weapon."

"I don't want a weapon. I want to rip you three apart with my bare hands." But he couldn't take such a risk and leave Adella open to another attack. He positioned himself between her and the men. "Still have your gun?" he called over his shoulder.

"You think you can hoodwink us?" One of the men snorted. "That we're blind as well as stupid? She ain't got no gun. And she wanted us to roll her. She was even grabbing her skirt, no doubt to raise it, when we found her."

Adella's footsteps told him she'd moved to stand beside him. He kept his gaze locked on the men.

"Can you hold this for me?" Her hand nudged his fist.

His fingers uncurled immediately at her bidding. She pressed something warm and cylindrical against his palm. He took it and raised his hand between him and the men, wondering what was so bloody important to give him. She'd handed him a knife.

"I'm a trifle shaky and require both hands." The hammer of a tiny gun clicked softly.

The men lurched back, hands raised. "Whoa, now! Don't get excited. We only wanted a little touch."

The blast ricocheted off the alley walls. So did the howling as the man who'd shoved up her skirt hunched over clutching his hand. Blood seeped through his fingers.

"You'll never be *touching* a woman with that hand again. Welcome to southern justice." Another click primed the second shot as she swung the gun toward the next man. "Your turn."

The men spun and dashed down the alley.

The knife she'd passed to him was still warm in his hand. "Where did this come from?"

"My boot." She retrieved the knife and returned it to its hiding place. "Men don't usually pay attention to that area when they're under a woman's skirt."

The knowledge that she'd nearly been raped, despite all his pitiful attempts to guard her, made him light-headed. He dropped his forehead into his hands. "Adella—"

She removed the distance between them, throwing her arms around his neck and pressing close. "Thank you for coming after me. For not giving up on me."

He held her tight. "Why would I give up on you?"

"You found me in Fergal's tent. He said—"

"I found you with a friend. One who, although I want to slug him for his comment, needs as much help as you."

She pulled free of his embrace.

"Don't be cross, lass. I didn't mean—"

"I can't stay out here any longer. It's too dark." Her golden irises were rimmed in white. Her gaze darted left and right, searching the shadows. She pressed the lantern into his hand. Derringer raised and cocked, she pulled him out of the alley.

Only after she'd entered the hotel, did she return her gun to its hidden pocket. When she opened the door to her room, he pulled back. He shouldn't go inside. With his worry for her riding him, he wouldn't be able to leave. And Adella had just been through hell. The last thing she needed was him pawing at her.

"You don't want to stay with me." Her voice cracked on the last word.

Regret flooded him. "Adella, I do. But I—"

"Thank you for coming to my rescue and returning me safely to my hotel." She crossed to stand by the window, moving as far from him as the room allowed. With trembling hands, she gripped the windowpane. "You're a good man."

"I want to be more than that. I want to be more than your guardian or even your lover." He pinched the bridge of his nose, struggling to rally his restraint, his common sense.

To hell with it.

He reached for the door. Stepping inside the room, he closed the door behind him. "I want to share everything, and I'm not leaving this room until we do."

Clutching the window, Adella strained to follow the sound of Cormac's quiet footsteps. He wanted to share— "Everything?" The word came out more squeak than coherent speech.

Cormac's fingers brushed her arm and she jumped.

The warmth of his hand retreated. "I want you to tell me about your brother. Then I want to undress you and make love to you in this room until the sun rises."

Longing squeezed her chest and left her lightheaded. "What if I become pregnant?"

"The prospect scares the hell out of me. But if you were happy and healthy, then nothing would give me greater joy than seeing you with my child. Would it..." his warmth returned, hovering near her shoulder, "... make you happy?"

"I think it would." Releasing the window, she leaned back into his hand. His strength and gentleness allowed her to breathe again. But her heart remained tight with uncertainty.

His hand on her shoulder tightened, then relaxed. "Then I think our sharing will work out well."

Would it? While she hated to speak of Declan, Cormac might be the only person who could understand her all-consuming guilt. Four of his sisters had died, had starved before his eyes.

"My brother—" Her throat constricted, but she forced herself to go on. "He— He died in a Union prison camp."

Sturdy, rock-hard arms enveloped her from behind with infinite tenderness. "I'm sorry, lass."

She welcomed his strength. "What is it like? Is it—painful?"

"Is what painful?"

Imaging Declan's suffering hurt like a railroad spike to the heart. "Starving to death," she whispered. "That's how my brother died as well."

Every one of his muscles—in his arms, shoulder, chest and abdomen—tensed around her, protecting her. "Adella, you don't want to know. Stop torturing yourself."

"Why? I deserve it. You were too young to save your sisters but you tried. And you were with them when they died. I was off spying for the Johnny Rebs."

"Did you know your brother was starving?"

"No, but—"

"That's where you learned to be a spy? In the war?"

She nodded.

His lips brushed the top of her head. "Well then, you were doing what you could to win the war and ensure your brother's release."

"Yes, but I wasn't there when he needed me most. I—" Guilt compressed her chest, stalling her breath again. She didn't want to tell Cormac about her last conversation with Declan, but she must. To repeat what she'd said would be like living it all over again. "I told him that...if he left home and joined the war...I wouldn't be there to help him when he needed me. I wanted to keep him from the fighting."

"Sounds like you were being a big sister trying to protect her brother."

Her breath left her in a harsh whoosh, somewhere between a laugh and a cry. "We were twins. I was only minutes older than Declan. Despite my words, he wrote me a letter every month during the war. But the things I said, that I wouldn't help him if he got in trouble, hung between us. Then he stopped writing when he was captured. When I heard he was in prison, I should've ridden straight north and bribed every Yankee I met into smuggling food into that death camp."

"He probably knew that wouldn't work."

"From the very beginning I should've guarded my words with him."

"I've learned that sisters can't help being bossy where their brothers are concerned." He gently tugged a lock of her hair.

"Do you still think about them?"

"Every day," he murmured.

"Will it stop?"

"I hope not. I want to remember them forever." His reply was swift and strong. Then his muscles rippled against her back as he blew out a breath. "I'm trying to recall only the good memories though."

"Like when you rode those stolen ponies with Molly?" She reached back and poked him in the ribs, hoping to brighten his mood.

He captured her hand and turned her to face him. The corners of his lips twitched. "I'm not the only thief in this room. You stole that telegram from Stevens' railcar." He pressed a kiss against her palm, sending shivers up her spine.

"Thanks to you Stevens got his telegram back the very next day," she teased.

"I also returned the landlord's ponies safe and sound. Did them all a favor. Those horses needed exercise and they enjoyed my attention." He nipped her hand.

Craving more of his attention, she pressed against him, molding her curves to his hard planes. They were so different, yet they fit so well together.

His lips brushed her ear. "I love you, Adella."

Joy pounded in her veins. "I love you, too."

With a growl, he carried her to the bed. Kneeling beside her on the mattress, he made swift work of removing her dress and corset. His fingers traced the neckline of her chemise. Ribbons unfurled. Cotton slid down her shoulders.

She caught its descent. "There's something I've dreamt of doing. Will you allow me a minute to indulge myself?" She made room for him on the narrow mattress.

His brows arched, but he lay down beside her without a word.

The tweed of his waistcoat and trousers were rough under her fingertips, his linen shirt only slightly softer. Beneath his clothing, his muscles were smooth and warm. They flexed and tightened at her lightest touch. She left no terrain unexplored.

"Time's up." His voice was hoarse, his breathing ragged as he reached for her chemise.

They removed the last of each other's garments together. His callused fingertips teased her inner thigh as he introduced her again to the pleasures from the barn. An ache blossomed deep inside her, as if the sun finally found her via his touch. Soon her breathing matched his. Then he sent her over the familiar, but still astounding, precipice.

Guiding her legs around his waist, he

pressed his hips to hers, and paused. "Remember what you told me in the barn?"

Confused tightened her brow. She'd told him many things.

He kissed her forehead. "That you'd never lain with a man before? Are you sure you want this?"

His hardness lay nestled between her legs, waiting to press home. She wasn't sure what she wanted. But she knew she didn't want time to reconsider, to retreat, to regret.

"You've never done this," he continued. "And I don't want to hur—"

She thrust herself against him, taking him to the hilt. The stab of pain startled her. She cried out. So did he.

He hovered over her, inside her. Motionless. Then he shuddered as if in pain as well. "I've hurt you. From the moment I saw you, I worried I would. I'm sorry." He gathered her close. His heart raced in time with hers. "But I'm not sorry about what comes next."

"What comes next?"

"When you're ready, you'll see."

"How long will that be?" She shifted against him, trying to get comfortable. Unexpected pleasure streaked through her. A groan rumbled deep in his chest and his hips rocked hers. Another all too fleeting burst of desire left her undulating with need.

Cormac moved with her, setting a pace she eagerly followed. Her need swelled, rising in surges, like waves on an ocean with no end in sight. Then her hunger spiked, sudden and overpowering as Cormac sent her over the edge and followed. She soared in weightless wonder, then drifted free of thought or care.

A lump of bed sheet irritated her spine. She hadn't thought she'd moved, but Cormac released her and rolled onto his side. Reaching beneath her, she pulled free his linen shirt.

A blush heated her cheeks as she recalled his words: *You'd make my oldest shirt look breathtaking.* What must he think of her now?

His fingers brushed her hand. "You want me to leave?"

She clutched the garment to her chest and turned away, employing her body as a shield. "The nights are still chilly. I hoped I might wear your shirt."

"Save it for the morning." He drew the covers over them. His torso and thighs formed a warm arc around her backside. "Tonight, I'm loath to allow anything to come between us." His arm curled around her, pulling her close again. "Thank you for finally deciding to share everything with me."

But she hadn't. Not everything. She hadn't told him about Helga and her dynamite, and Fergal and his plan to kill Parsons.

Fear, like a double-edged sword, prevented her from relaxing into Cormac's embrace. One edge of the blade held the old dread: if she told him everything, he might walk away from her in disappointment. But the other edge promised an even great terror: if she didn't speak now, she might lose him in the most painful way possible.

Cormac might die. He might die because of her.

She rolled to face him. "This afternoon when you asked what Helga said to me..."

"Aye?" He rubbed her back with a reassuring patience.

"She's decided that blowing up the track will help her keep her farm. She had dynamite in her basket."

A long silence elapsed before he replied. "The closest source of dynamite is the Katy's stockpile."

"Yes, she said her supplier was—"

"Fergal."

Feeling like a traitor, she lowered her gaze. "She wouldn't give me a name."

"But you suspected Fergal. You went straight to him." His embrace tightened, then relaxed. Not completely though. A tenseness, that hadn't been there before, remained. "Why seek him out?"

"I thought he might be one of the Irish outlaws who derailed the train."

Cormac released an extended breath and his stiffness vanished. "*To tyrants we'll not yield.*"

She nodded. "It's from the Confederacy's *Battle Cry of Freedom*." Her words poured out like stones, once freed, falling fast down a mountain. "Fergal told me that when Parsons arrives on the next train, he plans to kill him." Pulling out of Cormac's arms, she sat up. "I need to stop him and Helga too. If something happens because I didn't—"

He sat up beside her and hushed her worries with his lips. His kiss stole her breath and filled her heart with only one thing—the promise of love. "Nothing will happen," he whispered, resting his forehead against hers, "because we're united now. I can't lose with a partner like you on my side."

His lopsided smile tore at her heartstrings. She wasn't sure she felt the same way. With Cormac beside her, she had so much more to lose.

Chapter 9

Adella woke, warm and sated and content. An unusual feeling. A wonderful feeling. A feeling made possible because Cormac filled her bed and her thoughts.

Rolling over, she reached for him. Her arms found...emptiness. She bolted upright. Her gaze scoured her hotel room. Empty as well. Her happiness died as swiftly as a spring flower in a snowstorm.

Cormac had left her.

A flash of white atop her dresser caught her eye. A piece of paper? A letter! Scrambling free of the bedcovers, she tore across the room. Bold handwriting slanted across the page.

You are just as beautiful asleep as awake.

Could not bear to wake you. Gone to find Fergal and Helga.

Stay safe. STAY in this room where I can

find you.
Will return as soon as I can.
Cormac

Relief made her wilt against the dresser. He hadn't left her. Hard on the heels of her respite, alarm snapped her spine straight. Cormac didn't run from troubles or squander time sleeping in. He'd gone out to face their troubles head-on.

Snatching her dress from the floor, she donned the garment with fumbling fingers. The tiny enamel buttons thwarted her. The black bombazine mocked her. Widow's weeds for a lover she might never marry.

More than a lover. A loved one. If anything happened to Cormac— Her thoughts splintered, their razor-sharp edges left her gasping.

She forced herself to draw in a deep breath. Now more than ever she must not falter. She must find Cormac. She couldn't lose him like Declan. She wouldn't let him die. *To my very last breath, I pledge to keep you safe.*

She jerked on her drawers and boots. Too impatient to do more, she raced out of the room and down the stairs. Her unbound hair bounced on her back with each step. Her footfalls pounded out a drum roll. *Faster. Faster. Hurry. Hurry.*

At the bottom, stock-still behind his

counter, the hotel clerk's wide-eyed stare confirmed her crazy appearance. She sprinted across the lobby. Outside, she slammed to a halt on the front porch, wrapping an arm around a post for support.

Where to search first? If she chose wrong, it might mean the difference between life and death. Fergal was intent on killing Parsons. Would he hurt Cormac if he stood in his way? And Helga, would she care if anyone got in her way when she blew up the track?

The usual wave of people and wagons flowed by, as if nothing were different. Today, everything was different.

Down the far end of the nearest footpath, the uneven gait of a man snagged her attention. The man limped and leaned on a cane. Fergal.

Adella chased after him, side-stepping approaching pedestrians, darting around those heading in the same direction. She bumped elbows, trod on toes, apologized, but continued pushing forward. Three strides—and one pudgy storekeeper—away from reaching Fergal, a butcher in a stained apron halted to address the storekeeper. The two men stood with hands clasped, blocking the entire footpath.

She leapt into the mud. The sticky earth rendered it a monumental task to take a single step let alone hurry. She pinned her gaze on Fergal's back while he limped farther and farther away. Fergal paused at a corner, turned right and disappeared.

Finally clear of the men, she clambered back onto the footpath. With a prayer lodged in her throat, she sprinted forward and around the corner, Fergal stood not twenty paces away talking intently to a big blonde woman. Adella sprang back behind the nearest clapboard wall. Pressing her chest against the rough timbers, she stole a peak at her quarry.

Thank Dixie. She'd found both Fergal and Helga. And they hadn't seen her.

Unfortunately, the distance between her and them made it impossible for Adella to hear their conversation. At least Helga didn't have her basket. Relief, followed swiftly by anxiety, crashed over her like rogue waves. If Helga didn't have her dynamite, where was it? And where was Cormac?

Part of her hoped he was far away, at the worksite or even farther away with the survey team. Another part yearned for his stalwart presence and steadfast help. Once again, she was alone. And, although she couldn't hear anything Fergal and Helga said, the tension in their gestures spoke volumes.

Today was the day, the day someone died because of her failure to act. Just like with Declan. She couldn't wait for Cormac or for anyone else. She must do whatever it took. Right now.

Shoving away from her hiding place, she strode toward Fergal and Helga. A rumbling filled her ears. Suddenly, she was being jostled and pushed. A parade of dirty railroad workers and cleaner townsfolk surged past her, both on the footpath and in the mud. Their noise sharpened into individual chatter and footfalls.

Why weren't the workmen at the worksite? Why were the townsfolk on the street with them? It didn't matter. All that mattered was that their intrusion made it difficult to keep Fergal and Helga in sight. She mustn't lose them. She pushed through the crowd.

Fergal and Helga were moving as well now. Fergal had turned down another street, while Helga continued on with the crowd. Adella halted at the juncture separating the two, her gaze jumping between them. Who should she follow? Her decision might mean the difference between Parsons' life and death, or any number of the people around her.

"Adella," a familiar voice said behind her.

Turning, she found Kate Parsons gazing at her intently.

"I'm so glad I found you." Kate moved

closer. "I need your help."

Her help? Adella needed to *get* help not give it. Could she ask Kate to watch Helga or Fergal? No, not Fergal. What if he decided to hurt Kate to get back at her father?

"Can you bring your camera to the station?" Kate glanced at the crowd and smiled. "I'm organizing a—"

"Kate," Adella said, laying her palm on Kate's arm to gain her full attention. "I know this may sound peculiar, but I need you to follow Helga."

Kate shook her head so vigorously that several vibrant curls fell free of her tight coiffure. "I can't. Not now. I'm organizing a welcome reception for my father and an investor. They're arriving on the next train."

"The train?" Dread grayed the corners of Adella's vision. Under her hand, Kate's arm was a blessing, keeping her upright. "When does the train arrive?"

"In a few minutes. Adella... You don't look well. What's wrong?"

"I need you to keep Helga away from the station. She's planning to—" How could she explain without incriminating Fergal? She didn't want anyone hurt, including Fergal. She needed to stop him without getting him jailed. He wouldn't survive another prison. Not after what he'd suffered while incarcerated in Camp Douglas alongside Declan.

Fergal continued limping away, but Helga had halted. Adella hadn't lost track of either one. She still had time. But only minutes. The blasted train—

Helga had drawn a small knot of women around her. She towered over them, her face set in hard lines, her lips moving quickly.

"Dear lord," Kate breathed out. "Is Helga staging another protest? I can't let her do that. Not today." She strode toward the group.

"Kate, wait! I need to tell you—"

With a swift step and a steadfast gaze, Kate bore down on her target. Adella glanced in Fergal's direction. His silhouette was small and distant. What if he ducked down another pathway and she lost him for good?

She chased after him. Worry for Kate pricked her conscience, but she also felt a sense of relief. If anyone could stop Helga, it would be Parsons' determined daughter. And Adella had enlisted Kate's help without incriminating Fergal. Her luck was improving.

With the additional blessing of a footpath and street now vacant of people, she eliminated the gap between her and Fergal. Just behind him, she slowed to a walk and touched his sleeve. "Fergal—"

He spun around, the cane in his hand an arcing blur. She jumped back. Not soon enough. Pain exploded in her shoulder. She fell sideways, landing on her knees in the soft mud.

Fergal's narrowed eyes and pinched lips instantly opened wide with shock. "Del," he gasped in hoarse voice. Then he flung away his cane and leapt down to kneel beside her. "I'm sorry." He bowed his head and lifted her hands to his lips. "You're the last person I wanted to hurt."

Hope muted the pain in her arm to a dull ache. This was the Fergal she knew. She could save him. And if she did, she would save Parsons and everyone else.

A forlorn whistle called. Thin and drawn out. An approaching train whistle.

Fergal raised his head, tilting it toward the sound. "Don't follow me again." His voice was hard and low. "Stay out of this. Only one of us need sacrifice their future to avenge the past." He released her abruptly, and none too gently, and stood.

Her hope shriveled.

"Fergal!" The shout, a fierce but still feminine reprimand, had come from the footpath.

Eden stood there, fists on hips, glaring at Fergal. "Why are you abusing Miss Willows in such a fashion? That's not like you."

Fergal backed away from them. His cane lay in the mud, forgotten. So was his limp. "Return to your saloon, Eden, and take Adella with you," he said and then ran toward the station.

Bending down, Eden reached past the shoulder Fergal had struck to grasp Adella's other arm and help her onto the footpath. "How badly are you hurt?"

Adella avoided Eden's searching gaze. "Fergal didn't mean to hit me."

"Miss Willows," Eden replied in a tight voice. "Violent behavior such as that cannot be excused."

The train whistle came again. Shriller. Louder. Closer.

Adella swallowed hard. "You're right. The time for excuses is long gone. Can you find Cormac or the McGrady Gang?"

Eden's brows arched, but she nodded. "There's no time to waste I expect."

"There isn't."

"Where shall I instruct them to find you?"

"The station." Adella made a beeline for that destination.

Kate's welcome reception clogged the station's stairs, rendering it impossible to reach the platform. Adella only gained the second step. The boards vibrated beneath her feet as they'd done that first day in New Chicago when Cormac bounded up to rally his new recruits. Today, Kate, still dressed in her military jacket and trouser skirt, had assembled her own recruits—a group of civilians about to be blown apart by Fergal and Helga.

Suddenly, a handful of the McGrady Gang were behind her, then rallying around her.

"I need to reach the train," she told them.

With silent nods, they pushed through the throng, forging a path for her to follow. Above the heads of the crowd, the engine's stack appeared, belching acrid smoke as it led the train into the station. The McGrady Gang guided her to a prime spot where a private railcar—even more extravagant than Stevens'—halted in front of Fergal. Her mouth went dry and fear choked her.

At least Helga was nowhere in sight. Time remained to stop the violence. But now, rather than minutes, Adella only had seconds. The McGrady Gang withdrew a pace, giving her room while shielding her from the crowd. Stevens strode out of the throng and climbed the railcar's stairs. He reached for the door.

Dread sharpened her thoughts to one word. "Stop!" She took the final step and stood on the platform's edge beside Fergal.

An enthusiastic brass band struck up a tune and drowned her out. Stevens opened the door. A short, small-boned man with gray hair stepped through. Levi Parsons' eyes, as bright blue and determined as his daughter's, surveyed the crowd. Their clapping amplified the din. Parsons raised a hand in acknowledgment. Stevens stood behind him, smiling, his hand still on the door.

"You shouldn't have followed me here." Fergal kept his gaze fixed on the men on the train.

"You don't want to hurt Parsons."

"No, I don't."

Adella blinked, startled to have won his capitulation so easily.

"I want to hurt him." Fergal jabbed his finger at a second man who squeezed his hefty frame through the railcar door. The silver in his mutton-chop whiskers flashed as he straightened.

"Senator Moreton?" Adella shook her head. "He's not the one. He's a middleman. He gave me—" Dismay coiled around her heart. The senator had given her exactly what she'd asked for: knowledge in the form of irrefutable evidence. He'd given her Parsons' name on a Camp Douglas rations supply form. And after five years of searching she'd been too eager to question how easily Senator Moreton had produced the document.

"Tell me, Fergal. Tell me what you

know."

Fergal tilted his head toward her and pitched his voice low. "At first, it wasn't uncommon for Camp Douglas' supply wagons to arrive late. But after a while, they stopped arriving at all. Moreton came in their stead and slipped a fat envelope into the warden's eager hand. When the war ended, Moreton began a well-funded life in politics. A life built on the deaths of hundreds of expendable men, including Dec."

"But why frame Parsons?"

"Moreton's betting on both sides. He owns more stock in the Joy Line than in the Katy. With Parsons eliminated, his more profitable railroad is sure to win."

Standing between Stevens and Parsons on the railcar's rear step, Moreton surveyed the crowd. His bland smile remained fixed, until he spotted her and paused. His lips bowed with satisfaction, puffing out his side-whiskers like twin sails catching the wind. Then, as if she and he were strangers, his gaze resumed its leisurely stroll.

Senator Moreton was a chameleon. Just like her. He'd lied to her. He'd used her. She was merely a pawn in his game.

"I don't care about Parsons," Fergal said, his words tumbling out now. "He's a Yank and he's standing beside Moreton. Plus

Helga demanded my assistance with Parsons in exchange for her help with Moreton." He blew out a breath, then faced the train again. "It's too late to do anything differently. Our plans are in motion. They cannot be stopped."

No! She couldn't accept that. There was still time. Time to set things right. Time to stop the killing. Time to build a better future.

"Fergal, where's Helga?" she demanded.

"She left." Once again Kate stood behind Adella. The barrier of the McGrady Gang had proved no match for such a determined woman, especially one beaming with satisfaction. "Helga instructed the farm widows to proceed to the station without her. After she departed, I promised to arrange a meeting between the widows and my father. They agreed to delay their protest. The disaster has been diverted."

A frown chased away Kate's good humor. "But where's your camera, Adella? I need pictures. I want this welcome reception to be perfect for my father and his guest."

Adella's stomach did a slow, sickly lurch. Today was going to be far from perfect. The other widows may've been placated, but Helga wouldn't be. Adella scanned the crowd, searching for a tall blonde figure. Instead, Cormac's dark head and giant frame came up the stairs and then pushed through the crowed toward her. Eden followed in his wake.

Thank Dixie. And thank Eden too for finding Cormac. If anyone could help Adella mend this madness, it was Cormac. She wanted to meet him halfway and throw herself into his capable arms. She didn't want to face her struggles alone anymore.

Cormac's gaze locked on a point high above her. His face went white as chalk.

Adella spun around. Atop the railcar, Helga crouched in a pose, and clothing identical to the saboteur who'd unleashed the rails that first day. The only thing missing was the floppy hat.

Helga jumped down, her coat billowing to reveal a trio of cylindrical sticks strapped to her chest. Their brightly lit fuses dazzled Adella's eyes. Helga landed on the platform between Adella and Kate, her coat dropping to conceal her dynamite.

Shock held Adella immobile. The McGrady Gang stood poised as if ready to attack. Behind them, a few of the nearest townsfolk turned and stared. The rest continued clapping. Adella's heartbeat joined the band music accelerating toward a crescendo.

Fergal grabbed her arm at the same time as Helga seized Kate's.

"You need to leave, Adella." Fergal pulled her away from the two women.

Helga nodded, her gaze following them. "Tell everyone I was holding the railroad bigwig's daughter when the end came. He'll have my farm, but he won't have his daughter. That should make a powerful enough story for one of your photographs."

Like a climber losing her footing, Adella tumbled back to two days ago and the counsel she'd given Helga inside the missionary tent. *If a subject is powerful, then so is the photograph.* She'd started this. Now she must end it.

"I won't take that picture." Adella wrenched her arm out of Fergal's grasp. "And I won't go."

Cormac burst through the crowd and passed the McGrady Gang. He restrained Fergal in a headlock. The tuba and trombone cried their final notes. The cymbals smashed a resounding climax. And the crowd cheered in thunderous appreciation.

She threw herself at Helga. Helga stumbled under the onslaught. Kate slipped free, and Adella yanked open Helga's coat. The fuses had lost half their length.

The crowd's merriment had subsided to the chattering of magpies.

"She has dynamite!" Adella shouted into the lull. "She's going to blow up the train!"

Cormac shoved Fergal behind him and reached for her.

All sound stopped. The silence lasted as long as it took the crowd to inhale a collective breath of astonishment. Then a single scream split the air. And the crowd fled, running and shrieking as one.

"I wanted Parsons' daughter," Helga hissed. "You'll have to take her place."

A rock-hard restraint circled Adella's wrist. Helga's grasp was even more solid than when she'd grabbed Adella in the missionary tent or at the farm. Adella glanced down. Helga's hand didn't imprison her. A band of iron did. And a chain the length of her arm shackled her to an identical cuff around Helga's wrist.

Cormac's bellow filled her ears. "No!"

Behind him, eyes wide and jaws hanging, stood Kate, Eden, Fergal and the McGrady Gang. Beyond them were the backsides of the fleeing crowd. Only Cormac moved forward to help her. She couldn't let him.

She jerked sideways. Using all of her bodyweight, she yanked Helga with her and leapt off the platform. Her back struck the mud. Her lungs compressed, depriving her of air. Stars danced in her eyes as she stared at the sky high above. So bright. So blue. Where were the ever-present clouds? Was she dead? Was that why she felt so numb?

She turned her head. Helga lay beside

her with her coat open. During their fall, two of the sticks of dynamite had been snuffed out. Only one continued to sizzle on a next to nil fuse. One was enough.

Burn faster, she urged. Let it only be the two of us who die.

Mud splashed and sorrow flooded her. Cormac crouched between her and Helga. Shielding her with his body, he strained to pry the shackle from her wrist. The iron squealed in protest, then finally broke in two.

Cormac picked her up and ran.

The explosion roared in her ears, slamming Cormac against her, knocking them both to the ground. He didn't move. His stillness signaled her defeat. She'd come to town to ruin one man's life. Instead, she'd killed the man she loved.

She closed her eyes and prayed for her own death.

Chapter 10

Adella paced New Chicago's train platform waiting for the McGrady Gang to let her board the midday train for Emporia. The blasted Irishmen stood in a row, shoulder to shoulder, barring her way.

The boards vibrated under her feet as a single man bounded up the steps behind her. She halted, but kept her back to him. She couldn't bear to see the disappointment on Cormac's face. She deserved it though. Another death lay heavily on her conscience.

"Going somewhere, Miss Willows?" Cormac's deep brogue enveloped her, heating her chilled skin. She hadn't felt warm since she woken yesterday morning alone in the bed they'd shared. A bed where he'd shown his affection for her. That affection was gone. What other reason could there be for his continued absence following yesterday's barely averted disaster? Why hadn't he come to her hotel room last night?

"I'm going away," she replied. "I came to New Chicago for the wrong reasons. I should have come to save a man's life, not ruin one. Because of me, Fergal's dead."

A four-foot wide crater had gouged out the earth and destroyed the track south of the platform. A platform missing a sizeable chunk thanks to the power of a single stick of dynamite. Luckily she was heading north. But where she'd stop she didn't know, because it didn't matter. Nevertheless, she turned her gaze north, unable to face the damage she'd caused in New Chicago or the censure that must surely burn in Cormac's eyes.

Behind her, Cormac exhaled an extended breath. She wrapped her arms around her waist, struggling to hold onto her resolve not to look at him.

"Fergal wasn't your responsibility," he finally said. "He was mine. He may not have been with me and my men the day you arrived in town, but he was always one of us."

Had Fergal felt responsible for Cormac as well? After Cormac had covered her body with his, Fergal had done the same to Helga. But while Cormac had shielded Adella from the blast, Fergal had trapped the explosion between himself and Helga.

He'd died saving Adella and Cormac.

Parsons and Stevens had demanded explanations. Neither she nor Cormac had uttered a word about Fergal's involvement in Helga's murderous plan. And Cormac hadn't revealed Adella's role in harassing the Katy either.

She'd shared Fergal's compulsion to avenge Declan's death and, in her grief and single-mindedness, she allowed herself to do the unthinkable. She'd targeted an innocent man. Remorse clenched her chest in an unbreakable vise. But what hurt more was the realization that Fergal's grief had changed him so much, he'd willingly endangered every person on yesterday's train platform to gain his revenge.

Cormac must have sensed her rising turmoil because when he spoke again, his voice was firm. "Fergal was a hero. He saved your life and mine and, as far as the townsfolk need know, he sacrificed himself to save them as well."

She shook her head. "It should've been I who saved him. I should have—" Her thoughts spun as she searched for an answer. None came. "Fergal needed me. Just like Declan. I failed them both." And she'd failed Cormac too. She'd killed what might have been.

"Don't torture yourself, lass." His advice rumbled in her ears, low and soothing. "Let go of the past."

"What if I can't?" Her voice cracked on the last word. She squeezed her eyes shut.

He stroked the lock of hair that had escaped from her pins. He wound the curl around his finger. The warmth of his flesh, a hairsbreadth away from touching hers, made her lean toward him.

"You'll let go," he replied, "when you find something worth holding onto instead."

"Why didn't you come to me last night?" The question burst from her lips before she could stop it. She cringed in mortification.

"Oh, I wanted to. But Parsons is more determined than ever. He kept me and Stevens up half the night discussing his plans to ensure the Katy reaches the border first. Even though we're still running a hundred miles behind the Joy Line, Parson thinks that if we reach Ladore by May we might have a chance to win. All I could think was the only way I'd win was if you were still by my side in May."

By his side? He still wanted to be with her? A surge of hope made her spin to face him.

He towered over her. Her giant, dark-haired, silver-eyed Irishman clad in homespun tweed. He was perfect. Except for one thing. He held her valise in his hand.

She gaped at it, speechless.

"I thought—" He cleared his throat and held out the bag for her to take. "I thought you might need it."

"Why?" Since they'd first met, her valise had come between them. Now he wanted her to have it back? He was willing to erect another barrier between them? Disappointment compressed her lungs to the point of suffocation. She snatched the valise from his grasp and hurled it as far as she could, which wasn't far enough.

"I don't want it anymore." With her breath lodged in her chest, her voice came out ragged. She started pacing again. Two strides left, then right and left again. "It can stay here, for all I care."

Cormac's hands claimed her shoulders, anchoring her in place. Her heart raced with yearning while his brow furrowed. Why did she always hurt the ones she loved?

He leaned closer. "Why not stay as well?"

"Aye, you should stay," said one of the McGrady Gang.

"Mac will be impossible to be around if you don't."

"It wouldn't feel right with you gone, miss."

She glanced over her shoulder at Cormac's gang and the train behind them. Charcoal smoke billowed from its stack. The train was ready to leave.

Cormac's grip tightened. "You can't deny what you've heard. You're needed here. Eden could use a friend as well. And Kate too."

Adella released a shaky laugh. "Kate hates me for what I nearly did to her father."

"No, she doesn't." Cormac's reply held the same resolute tone she'd heard him use when rallying his men.

His thoughtfulness humbled her. She hung her head. If only there was a chance for friendship between her and Kate. But that was more than she could hope for. More than she deserved.

Cormac crooked a finger under her chin and raised her head until she stared directly into his eyes. "If you won't stay for friendship, stay for love."

She blinked in disbelief. "You still love me?"

"More than ever." His frown deepened. "I'm also increasingly afraid that I can't keep you safe."

The tightness gripping her chest vanished. "On that score, I have no fear at all." She hooked a finger around the top button of his waistcoat and pulled. "Come closer, giant."

He reached down and swept her off her feet and into his arms. Behind her, the McGrady Gang erupted in whistles and cheers.

"You realize—" she laid her cheek against his chest, luxuriating in the steady beat of his heart, "—life with me won't be a fairytale."

"I know," he whispered against her ear, then gently tugged her hair. "It'll be better."

She laughed, this time with her entire heart and soul. Visions of enemies faded. Maybe one day they'd disappear entirely. Maybe not. The thought didn't distress her as it once had.

As long as there was room for her in Cormac's heart, the future held promise.

The End

DEDICATION

Thank you Elisabeth and Jennifer for dreaming of a railroad-themed Western anthology and granting me the honor of working with you.

Thank you to my writing friends at VIC, GVC, and RWA® who—over many years—have helped me become a better writer.

Special thanks to Nora Snowdon and Lynda Bailey who faithfully reviewed every page of *Adella's Enemy*.

Finally, and as always, thank you to my mom, sister, and nephew.

~ *Jacqui Nelson*

PASSION PRIZE ANTHOLOGY

Outlaws, soldiers, and spies bedevil the Katy Railroad as construction crews race to reach Indian Territory before their rival. The prize—a fortune in land rights for the wining line. Stakes are just as high for three women whose lives hinge on the outcome.

If you enjoyed *Adella's Enemy*, why not try the two other novellas in the *Passion's Prize* anthology…
Eden's Sin by Jennifer Jakes and
Kate's Outlaw by E.E. Burke.

ABOUT THE AUTHOR

Jacqui Nelson writes historical romantic adventures set in the American West and Victorian London. Her love of Western stories came from watching classic Western movies while growing up on a cattle farm. Her passion for Victorian London wasn't far behind and only increased when she worked in England for four years and explored the nooks and crannies of London on her weekends. She currently lives on the west coast of Canada. She is a Romance Writers of America® Golden Heart® winner and three-time finalist.

CONTACT JACQUI AT

www.JacquiNelson.com
www.facebook.com/JacquiNelsonBooks
www.facebook.com/JacquiNelsonAuthor
www.twitter.com/Jacqui_Nelson

AFTERWORD

Thank you so much for reading *Adella's Enemy*.

I loved writing Adella and Cormac's story, and I hope you enjoyed reading it. If you purchased this book on Amazon, I would ask a favor—please take a few minutes to leave an honest review.

Authors enjoy hearing that readers like their stories. Other readers enjoy hearing about stories they might find interesting. If you enjoyed a book, help share it with another reader.

www.amazon.com/author/jacquinelson

OTHER BOOKS BY
Jacqui Nelson

Coming soon, the Golden Heart®
nominated Westerns...
Between Heaven & Hell
Between Love & Lies

Turn the page for an excerpt from
BETWEEN LOVE AND LIES

Chapter 1

South of Dodge City, Kansas—May 1876

The cattle were destroying everything: the tiny apple tree she'd sheltered in the wagon during the long, sweltering journey from Virginia; the fence she'd devoted weeks to repairing over the winter with scraps of deadwood; the vegetable garden she'd sown during the first whisper of spring and painstakingly coaxed to life every heartbeat since.

All trampled, devoured, gone.

Sadie glared at the beasts, eyes burning with tears of hopeless rage. They were thin, ugly creatures, spindly legs culminating in cloven hooves, heads wielding heavy horns that twisted out of their skulls in long spikes. Texas longhorns, the Devil's helpers. In the middle of them rode Lucifer himself, sent straight up from Hell to torment her and tear away everything she'd slaved to build.

She tracked the long-legged, solid-built cowboy as he steered his horse through the milling beasts, angling toward her and her father—and their sod house which, she realized with a jolt of dismay, was also in danger of being leveled by the heaving mass of cattle. The intruder, similar to all the other Texas drovers, was covered in a layer of trail dust so thick it hung on him like a second skin. But it was one of the only things he and the other men had in common. While the rest hollered and cracked whips over the backs of the beasts in their charge—trying to persuade them to return to the trail—this man urged his mount through the river of hide and horn, making a beeline for her.

It infuriated her that he was so silent, that he could guide his horse with remarkably little effort. As the distance between them shortened, unease crept up her spine. His gaze was unwavering, never leaving her.

She swallowed, tightened her fingers around the ancient shotgun clutched at her side, and concentrated on her anger and frustration, transferring them from the longhorns to settle solely on him. She did not want him to come any closer. Yanking the shotgun up to her shoulder, she took aim. The cowboy straightened in his saddle but otherwise did not acknowledge her hostile action. Nor did he slacken his pace; if anything, he bore down on her even faster.

Damn him to hell. Her finger tightened on

the trigger.

Something slammed down on her shotgun, pitching the rusted barrel earthward. The buckshot tore a savage gouge out of the clay in front of her, kicking up a cloud of dust. The blast rocked her and forced her to stumble back.

Her father's red face inserted itself between her and the cowboy. With a curse, he jerked the weapon from her numb hands.

As she stood gawking at him, the cattle, spooked by the shotgun blast, bolted—fast and in every direction. Her father sprinted toward their lone plow horse, vaulted onto its back and galloped away from her and the cattle.

Typical. She shouldn't have expected anything different from him. He'd thought only of securing his own safety. He'd abandoned her alone and unarmed in the center of the herd.

I'm going to be trampled. I'm going to die.

Time suspended as she contemplated her life ending. She felt nothing. All her hard work had been obliterated in a blink, and she could not summon the will to fight back, to face the prospect of starting over. If this was the end, so be it.

The bawling cattle and thundering hooves were deafening. The heat of their breaths hit her first, then their bodies. Walloped square in the chest, her lungs compressed and she was knocked off her feet. But the surge did not wash over her. Instead, a solid hand caught her about the waist, jerking her up until she crashed into an immovable wall.

She sucked in air and immediately wished she hadn't. Pain pierced her ribs. Dust billowed and shrouded the air, blinding her. Through slitted eyes she realized her leather-clad perch was already covered in a thick blanket of dust...and she was being pressed tightly against it. Frowning, she struggled to raise her head and discovered a square, beard-stubbled jaw directly above her.

Lucifer—in the disguise of a Texan cowboy—held her in his lap while waves of cattle buffeted his mount, his grip on her solid but not bruising as he guided them to safety. When they had cleared the beasts and the noise level dropped a notch, he peered down at her. Eyes like warm whiskey stared at her from an angular face etched with concern.

"Are you hurt?" His voice was low and ragged; his breath fanned out in bursts, caressing her face.

Her world tilted and the air once more left her lungs. She forced herself to remember he was responsible for destroying everything she held dear. Anger flooded her, pushing away all other thought, the same way his herd had swept away her dreams.

She curled her fingers into a fist and hit him as hard as she could in the stomach. Pain ricocheted up her arm. He didn't budge. He merely blinked, his brows lowering. Infuriated by his lack of response, she unleashed a flurry of hits, striking him with her fists, elbows and feet.

Beneath them, his horse spooked, whinnied shrilly and reared up.

Blind to everything but her need to make him hurt as much as she did, she launched her entire body at him. They tumbled from the horse and struck the ground hard, him landing first on his back, her on top of him. His breath left him in a grunt of surprise, but his hands remained locked around her waist. She scrambled to her knees before he pulled her back down. Twisting and turning, she struggled in vain to break free of his grip.

"Hold still. I'm trying to help you. You're gonna get us both killed."

His voice caught her off guard, stilling her. The tone was rough and demanding but edged with a note of pleading. Its undercurrent tugged at her.

Bewildered, she shook her head, refusing to yield to him. "Trying to help?" she yelled, slamming a fist down on his chest. "Do you know how long it took me to plant that garden? Or build that fence?" She hit him with her other hand. Exhausted, she wondered if he even felt her punches, which angered her beyond reason. "You've destroyed my entire life!"

She pounded out her fury on him until she couldn't lift her arms. When she stilled, he shocked her by gathering her close, drawing her into the curve of his body, pulling her head down onto his shoulder. His touch was gentle and reassuring; his palm cradled the back of her head, while his fingers smoothed the wild tangle of her hair.

His tenderness was her undoing. No one had held her with such care in a long time. Not since her mother had died. Great sobs shook her and she hid her face in his shoulder, unable to stop her tears.

He remained motionless until her shoulders ceased shaking, then stroked the rough pads of his thumbs across her cheeks and tucked her snarled tresses behind her ears. Her stomach squeezed into a knot and she hunched her shoulders, burrowing her nose into the tear-dampened wool of his jacket. The smell of him—masculine and earthy—infused her senses with longing.

"If I could undo the damage, I would," he whispered against her ear, his voice soft and husky. Silk and sand. Together with his breath, hot against her skin, it unleashed a storm in her belly, like a herd of pronghorn antelopes spying a mountain lion.

She jerked away, scrambling off him. This time he didn't move to stop her. She didn't go far, though. She didn't have the energy. Sitting stiff-backed beside him, she stared blankly at the rubble that had once formed her home. The salt of her tears stung her skin and her eyes ached, mirroring the pain in her soul.

His stiff leather chaps creaked as he stood

and stepped closer. The din associated with the longhorn herd had faded, the cattle having returned to the trail, once again heading north toward Dodge. The drover didn't follow them, nor did he touch her. The heat of his body did, though, intensifying the strange fluttering in her stomach.

"It can be rebuilt." The words were spoken plainly, without a trace of doubt. Maybe such things were possible in his world, but not in hers.

A bitter bubble of laughter burst from her, and she bit down on her lip. She wouldn't let him see how much he'd hurt her. See that a scream was building inside her. One so big that, if she let it out, she was certain she would shatter. "Easy for you to say."

He sighed. "I know it won't be easy, but I can't undo what's happened."

You have no idea! her mind screamed as she watched her father steer the aging swayback mare toward them.

She lurched to her feet. Behind her, the cowboy placed a callused hand under her elbow but she shrugged off his hold, refusing to look at him. Instead, she glared at her father and dreaded what was certain to come. She knew him too well—his manipulative mind, his greed and his lack of love for her, his own flesh and blood.

But when her father reached them, it was the cowboy who spoke first. "It's a right shame, my herd moving through your homestead like that, Mr.—?"

"Sullivan. Timothy Sullivan. And yes, it is."

What her father lacked in stature, he made up for with a classically boned face and thick hair gone white before of its time. With looks like that and his smooth-talking tongue, he really should have pursued a career in the theater. Then maybe he could have made a contribution to their meager funds instead of being a drain on whatever she earned. Unfortunately, he was more interested in drinking and gambling.

He eyed Sadie briefly, then turned to the man standing next to her, his familiar features settling into a look of mournful loss. "Me and my daughter worked hard building the place."

Liar!

He hadn't expended a single minute on their farm. He'd left that all up to her. She cringed at his charlatan nature, knowing he'd ply the cowboy with a consummate actor's skills, trying to extract as much compensation as he could for something he had no part in creating.

The cowboy surprised her again. "I'll compensate you fairly for your loss, Mr. Sullivan. It's the least I can do for you…and your daughter."

Not wanting to see any more, she turned away but couldn't block out the scrape of his footsteps, the jingle of his spurs, as he approached her father. They rang harsh against the tender earth of her home. He murmured something, deep and gravelly, that she couldn't catch. But she heard the surprise in her father's gasp.

"You are most generous, sir!"

She spun around. A tall stack of greenbacks rested on her father's soft, white palms. Her heart plummeted and the starch went out of her spine. She looked at the cowboy, her eyes burning with unshed tears.

His brows drew together and he took a step toward her. She took one back, shaking her head, forcing all the emotion from her heart and, she hoped, from her face. She turned and kept moving away from him, to where her home had once stood.

Giving that much money to a compulsive gambler was a sure-fire recipe for disaster. It would be gone come morning...and so would her future.

Made in the USA
Charleston, SC
25 April 2015